THE BAR WAS SMOKY AND CROWDED.
CHANCE AND VUKOVICH SLIPPED
INTO A BOOTH.

"We're at the same point everyone gets to with Rick Masters," Chance said after they were served. "Nowhere. He's too slick for surveillance."

"So what do we do now?"

"Either hang up our jocks and admit he's untouchable or be slicker than he is," Chance said.

"Have anything in mind?"

"A wiretap on his phone would do the trick."

"There's no way we can get a legal court order for a phone bug . . ."

"You're right. The only way to do it is to be resourceful."

"Resourceful? . . . You're talking about getting fired and possibly ending up in the joint if we get caught. You're talking about commiting a felony."

"That is *if* we get caught," Chance said. He took a drink and wiped his mouth with the back of his hand . . .

Pinnacle books by Gerald Petievich

MONEY MEN
ONE-SHOT DEAL
TO DIE IN BEVERLY HILLS
TO LIVE AND DIE IN L.A.

GERALD PETIEVICH
TO LIVE AND DIE IN L.A.

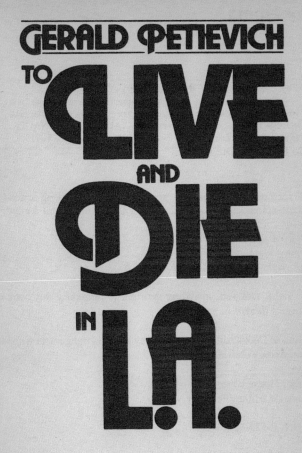

PINNACLE BOOKS NEW YORK

For Emma

This is a work of fiction. Any similarity to persons living or dead is purely coincidental . . . and exists solely in the reader's mind.

TO LIVE AND DIE IN L.A.

Copyright © 1984 by Gerald Petievich

Pinnacle Books edition, published by special arrangement with Arbor House Publishing Co.

Arbor House edition published in 1984
Pinnacle edition/February 1985

ISBN: 0-523-42301-2

Can. ISBN: 0-523-43305-0

Printed in the United States of America

PINNACLE BOOKS, INC.
1430 Broadway
New York, New York 10018

9 8 7 6 5 4 3 2

TO LIVE AND DIE
IN L.A.

CHAPTER ONE

A mellow-voiced weatherman on the car radio predicted rain.

Rick Masters changed the station as he steered carefully across the Vincent-Thomas Bridge which spanned a portion of the murkiness known as the Port of Los Angeles. As he reached the tollbooth at the entrance to Terminal Island he realized that it was dark enough for headlights. He pulled the headlight switch on the polished wooden dashboard of the Rolls-Royce, turned right onto Ferry Street and cruised along the industrial thoroughfare past canneries and marine salvage yards toward the water. Though he didn't need it to find his way, at the end of the street was an inconspicuous metal sign, the kind used to mark such places as insignificant historical landmarks. The sign read: Terminal Island Federal Prison. He swerved in the direction of the arrow on the sign and followed a narrow road which led to a parking lot in front of the dingy, brownstone administration building.

The compound was fortified by a high chain-link-topped-with-concertina-wire fence which extended from either side

of the administration building back to the heavy black rocks
at the water's edge. To the left of the edifice was a gun tower
equipped with a large spotlight which he remembered fanta-
sizing about while he served time there more than ten years
ago. At night, he'd imagine himself crawling effortlessly to
the top of the gun tower and escaping by running straight up
the beam of light and into the black Pacific sky. The phan-
tasm had occurred to him, as far as he could remember, each
and every day during the three year and four month stretch.
Crazy.

He parked the car, flicked on the interior light and
checked his appearance in the rearview mirror. Unlike the
prison white sidewalls fashioned by the Terminal Island bar-
ber years ago, his hair was styled and blow-dried. With his
shaded French-frame eyeglasses he was sure that none of the
turnkeys would recognize him. As he climbed out of the
Rolls, he could feel the rain in the air. He pulled on a three-
quarter-length black leather jacket and headed toward the
administration building.

Inside, a large reception area that he used to mop as a
trustee looked exactly as he remembered it: tidy, but unsani-
tary. The floor was drab brown tile and the gas-chamber-
green walls were decorated with framed photos of the
president and some gray-haired prick who was the current
director of federal prisons. Though the reception area was
the only place for visitors to wait, there were neither sofas
nor chairs.

At the opposite end of the room, a sallow-faced young
guard sat at a small desk reading a magazine. The desk was
arranged perpendicular to a door of bars which Rick Masters
knew was the only way in or out of the prison. Masters approached the guard. As he did so, he noticed that the title of
the magazine was *Heavy Metal*.

"Visitor?" the guard said without looking up.

"Yes, officer," Masters said in a supplicatory tone.

The guard pointed to a stack of printed forms on the corner of the desk. Masters picked up a pen attached to the desk leg by a string and filled out one of the forms.

NAME OF INMATE TO BE VISITED: Carmine Falcone
VISITOR'S NAME AND AGE: Albert L. Truman—43
ARE YOU RELATED TO THE INMATE? Yes
RELATIONSHIP: Cousin

Rick Masters handed the form to the guard.
The guard held out his hand. "I.D.," he said.
"Pardon me, sir?"
"You got some I.D.?"
"Certainly," Master said as he reached for his wallet. He took out the Truman driver's license and handed it to the guard. As the guard noted the number of the operator's license on the printed form, Rick Masters felt a sense of excitement, a controlled cock-and-balls innervation. He was showing his work.

The guard handed back the license. Though Masters felt like sighing, he simply put the license back in his wallet. The guard opened a bound volume of computer printouts and leafed through to Falcone's name. He wrote another number on the form, then picked up the phone. "One in for F sixteen zero four two three, a relative," he said. As the guard set the receiver down, the door of bars opened slowly into the wall. "Down the hall to the visitor's room," the guard said. "In the room sit at window number six. Use the phone. Visiting hours are over in a few minutes."

"Yes, sir," Rick Masters said. He stepped past the door. As he followed the guard's instructions he heard the heavy door slowly slide closed behind him. He entered a steel-walled room fashioned with a row of numbered glass windows which, like urinals, were partitioned from one another. Each window was furnished with a black wall phone. Rick Masters sat down in a chair facing window number six. He remembered being called to the opposite side of the window years ago for visits from his wife whom he'd divorced shortly after being released. He remembered how, after each of the monthly strained small-talk sessions, he'd walk the yard, thinking about the time he'd fucked her on the hood of his car as it was parked in a busy restaurant parking lot in Beverly Hills. Oddly, passersby had ignored them. There had been other times like that in those days, including getting her off in the cramped lavatory of a 707 during a flight to Las Vegas and on the crest of a ski run at Aspen. But the hood of the car incident was his favorite during the stretch. It had been his idea.

Like an aquarium fish, Carmine Falcone, a dark-featured man of Masters's age, suddenly appeared at the window. As he sat down he set a pink Pepto-Bismol bottle on the counter in front of him. It was half full. He grabbed the phone off the hook. Rick Masters did the same.

"Hello, partner," Falcone said in his New York accent.

"How are you making it?" Masters said in a fatherly tone. He lit a thin brown cigarette with a gold lighter.

"Forget the small talk. You know how I'm making it. I'm making it like every other swinging dick in this place makes it. Day by motherfucking day."

Masters nodded at the medicine bottle. "Ulcer acting up?"

Falcone nodded. "I want to know when you're going to get me out."

Masters took a puff of the cigarette. To give himself an extra moment to think before he answered, he changed hands with the phone receiver. "Grimes the mouthpiece let me down. He told me, he *promised* me that the fix was in with the federal judge. He kept telling me to be patient, that he would have you out soon. He kept assuring me that the fix was in. That's why I kept sending word for you to keep your shirt on. Grimes used to be an assistant U.S. attorney . . . a federal prosecutor. I believed him when he told me he had the connections. I took the man at his word."

"Okay, so I kept my shirt on," Falcone said. "I've copped a plea like Grimes told me to and now I've been sentenced to five fucking years for getting caught carrying a package of fifties. Now what?"

"I want you to be patient a little longer," Masters said.

"The federal attorneys are frothing at the mouth to get you. They want me to testify before a grand jury. Even the warden called me in for a soft-soap session. He offers to make me a trustee if I'd cooperate with the Feds against you. Everybody knows I'm your partner. Everybody knows I'm the one that helps you print. It's right in my prison file that you and I met while working in the prison print shop years ago."

"What did you tell them?"

"I tell 'em all to go pound sand. What the fuck do you think I tell them?"

"I didn't mean it like that," Masters said.

"But I'm telling you to your face right now that I'm not going to do the time, partner. I got caught carrying for *you*. I told you I didn't want to, but you didn't trust anyone else. It's always been that way. I'm the guy who buys the paper. I cart the press. I help with the plates. I cut the bills when they're printed. I carry the packages. I never complain. Well, now it's my turn for some motherfucking consideration. I want out and I'm going to do whatever it takes to get out."

Rick Masters bit his lip, watched Falcone closely.

"Do you understand what I'm laying on you?"

"I think you're telling me that if I don't get you out, you're going to the grand jury."

Carmine Falcone swallowed twice. "The last thing in the world I want to be is a rat. You know that. But I'm not going to sit here beating my meat for five years. If it comes to me or you, then it's going to have to be you. I can't do five years."

Masters looked him in the eye. "I'm giving you my word you won't have to do the whole nickel in here."

"What does that mean?"

"It means that everything is not lost. Grimes tells me that there still is a very good chance that the judge will go for letting you out on an appeal bond."

"Then what the hell is he waiting for?"

"This is something I can't answer."

"Doubletalk," Falcone said. "You're giving me doubletalk just like that shyster Grimes has been giving me doubletalk." He leaned close to the glass. "I helped you get where you are today. I've taken heat for you. You owe me."

"Grimes is the best lawyer money can buy. He's working on the arrangements. It'll be either an appeal bond or a sentence reduction. One way or the other he's going to get you out."

"And the check is in the mail," Falcone said sarcastically.

"I'm doing everything I can," Masters said after a pause.

"What about your pal Max Waxman?" Falcone said. "He's a lawyer. Can he help?"

"That's who I came down to talk about," Masters said. "Max the Money Man."

"What about him?"

"He was your last stop before the airport on the day you were arrested."

Carmine Falcone was silent for a moment. "What are you trying to tell me?" he said in a deliberate manner.

"He said that you never delivered the package to him."

A look of dismay suddenly swept over Falcone's face. "What do you *mean* he says he never got it? I walked right into his law office with a suitcase. I counted out the six hundred thousand right there on his desk. I had it wrapped in ten-thousand-dollar packages just like you told me. He put it in the safe he has right behind his desk. What do you *mean* he says he never got it?''

"He said you called him and postponed delivery. The next thing he heard was that you got arrested at the airport.''

"He's a lying son of a bitch. He must have done some quick thinking when he heard I took a fall. Like who would know how much funny money the Feds took away from me at the time of the arrest? That's what he must have figured.''

"What did you talk about with him when you dropped the package off that day?''

Falcone shrugged. "Nothing in particular. I might have said something about the problem we had with the plates for the serial numbers . . . small talk.''

The men gazed at each other through the thick glass without speaking. "Did you tell him where you were going?'' Masters finally said.

"Where I was going?''

"Where you were headed from his office?''

Falcone leaned on the receiver. His eyes closed as if he were trying to concentrate. "I think I told him I was in a hurry to get to the airport. I told him about making a run to Las Vegas for you.''

"Then he's the one who did you,'' Masters said. "He ratted you to the Feds.''

"But when they arrested me the T-men said the tip came from somebody in Las Vegas.''

"The Feds always say shit like that. They like to confuse people. He dropped a dime on you to screw me out of the six hundred grand.''

"Goddamn,'' Falcone said. "I think you're right. Damn, I'll kill him when I get out. I'll waste the motherfucker. May God strike me dead if I don't waste him. He set me up. He fucking set me up.'' He flinched as a guard tapped him on the shoulder.

"Visiting hours are over,'' the guard said. He strolled back toward a door.

"Don't forget about me," Falcone said.

"I won't. You have my word on that."

Both men set the receivers back on hooks.

Rick Masters stood up, moved to the door and down the hallway. The door of bars slid open. He ambled through the reception area to the front door.

The rain started just as he drove out of the parking lot. It came down in sheets as he drove back across the bridge and north on Harbor Freeway. In the cozy atmosphere of the Rolls-Royce he thought about his visit with Falcone.

Twenty miles later, as he made the transition from the Harbor to the Hollywood Freeway, a motorcyclist in the next lane was bumped by a van. The rider spilled to the pavement. The van squealed brakes and with the sound of crashing metal, spun out of control into the guard rail.

Rick Masters stepped on the accelerator to avoid the mess.

He drove north through Hollywood via the freeway, then turned off at an exit which led him to Studio City. He passed through a suburban business area and turned toward the foothills on Mulholland Drive. The upgrade led him into an area made up of homes which were either hidden off access roads, balanced by struts on hillsides, or, like his own, built on the crest of a turn to provide a view of the San Fernando Valley.

As he turned into the driveway the all-news radio station was announcing a list of intersections which were blocked due to flooding. He knew that's the way it was in L.A., a little rain or wind and the whole city fell apart.

The living room, which his girl friend, Blanca, had decorated in muted tones of brown and red, was warm. The television was turned to a quiz program.

Blanca was asleep on the sofa. She was a dark-complexioned woman with high cheek bones, full lips, Aztec eyes (a tiny teardrop tattoo decorated the corner of her left eye) and a figure that had given her top billing at Bodies Unlimited, a

Sunset Boulevard strip club that changed its name every time it was raided by the vice cops. She wore a pair of form-fitting jeans and a low-cut western-style silk blouse that didn't quite contain her ample bust. She started awake. ''I was having a bad dream,'' she said in her East L.A. barrio dialect. As usual, her face was void of expression, her brown eyes doleful, squawlike.

Masters walked over to the liquor cabinet and asked her what it was about.

''I was onstage doing my thing and people in the audience were burning me with cigarettes,'' she said sleepily. ''Serena once told me she always wrote down her dreams. She kept them in a little book.''

Rick Masters opened the liquor cabinet, pouring himself a Crown Royal whisky. ''Who's Serena?'' he said before he took a sip.

''She was in the show . . . the one who did the body paint thing.''

''Uh.''

Blanca struggled to sit up. With delicate cocoa-colored hands, she lit a cigarette. ''Did you go down there?'' she asked.

He nodded and took another sip of whisky.

''What did Carmine say?''

''He said Max did it to us.''

''Who do you believe . . . him or Max?''

''At the trial the Feds testified that when Carmine was arrested all he had on him was forty grand. That was exactly what was in the package I gave him to take to Las Vegas.''

''So Max *did* get the six hundred thousand?''

''That's what it looks like.''

''I wonder what he did with it?'' she said.

''Sold it, of course. What do you *think* he would do with it? Stick it up his ass?''

Angrily, she blew smoke at him. ''Excuse me for living,'' she said, reclining back on the sofa.

He finished the drink.

"Max called again while you were gone."

"Max rips me off for six hundred grand and then keeps calling me for more just like nothing happened . . . balls. Real balls."

"He's probably doing it to make it look like everything is the same as before."

"Did anyone else call?" he said, ignoring the self-evident remark.

"Just Reggie."

"What did he want?"

"An ounce of coke. He said he's having a party tomorrow night for the cast of his TV show."

"So what did you tell him?"

"I told him you'd get back to him."

"Do we have an ounce?"

"We still have three ounces left in the safety deposit box."

Rick Masters walked over to the sofa, sat down next to her. Leaning back, he rested his head on the top of the backrest. "Deliver him an ounce and charge him the same as before," he said. For the next few minutes he just stared at the ceiling. The television was a jumble of voices and sounds. He heard a quiz show host with a snappy, tenor voice asking the question, *"What European country is also known as the Emerald Isle? For five hundred dollars, your answer please."* Again he reviewed his conversation with Falcone. The thoughts mixed with flashes of memory: his mother taking him to the L.A. County Jail to visit his father; his father asking him how he was doing in school.

Masters reached to an end table and picked up a princess phone. He dialed a number he knew by heart. A woman answered. "Law offices," she said.

"This is Rick. I'd like to speak with Bob Grimes."

The phone clicked twice. "What did your friend have to say?" Grimes asked when he picked up the phone.

"He said he wants out."

"Did you tell him I can't get him out?"

"The man wants out."

"I've done everything humanly possible and he should realize that. At this point there may be no other alternative but to serve some time. Even if the judge grants an appeal bond, it's just a postponement. He was caught holding forty grand and he's going to have to serve his time. I've explained this to him more than once in great detail."

"Do you think he's going to cave in on me?"

"If he does, what can he give them?"

"Everything."

There was silence for a moment. Grimes cleared his throat. "I see no *easy* way out of the problem, if you know what I mean."

Rick Masters set the phone down.

"Do we have problems, baby?" Blanca said.

"Two big ones."

"Max and Carmine."

"That's right," he said as he stood up and strolled to the steamy bay window. The street gutters were overflowing: brownish rivers rushing downhill. In a brick planter which lined the driveway, a line of petunias the gardener had planted a few days earlier were now bent over, covered with mud. He stood there staring out the window.

"What are you gonna do?" Blanca said.

"I want you to go borrow a car."

"From who?"

"Go over and borrow one of Reggie's cars. Come straight back here."

"Right now?"

He turned and glared at her.

"Okay, okay," she said as she slithered off the sofa and got to her feet. She left the room and returned a minute later wearing a coat and carrying an umbrella. "How do I get over there?"

"Call a taxi," he said as he continued to stare at the rain.

"What are we going to do?" She opened a small loose-leaf book that was next to the phone, dialed a number and asked for a taxi.

"Take care of one of our problems," he said. The sound of his voice seemed to reverberate against the window.

CHAPTER TWO

Outside, the wind whipped and swirled the rain.

John Vukovich sat in a chair facing the window in the priest's study. There were no lights on in the musty-smelling room. Because it was dark, he knew he couldn't be seen by anyone who happened to look up from the rain-slick Wilshire Boulevard below.

Vukovich stood up. He opened the window and, leaning forward, held his hands outside for a moment. The droplets which tickled his palms were, like L.A.'s monotonous year-round weather, lukewarm. He touched wet fingers to his eyelids, then closed the window. He held his wrist closer to the window's reflected street-light illumination and checked the time. It was almost 7 P.M.

For what seemed like the millionth time, he surveyed the scene across the street; a modest one-story professional building with a decorative wood facade. Venetian blinds covered a bay window that faced the street. The lights were on inside. The building was situated between a small parking lot and a Mission-style apartment building; on the corner to the left was a service station.

He sat down again. Though he could hear his partner pacing the hallway outside the study, Vukovich felt utterly alone. Probably, he thought, because nothing much had happened all day . . . hell, the rain itself had been a welcome event. Nothing, that is, except that Max the Money Man Waxman had remained in his law office rather than leave at six-thirty as he usually did.

As he sat transfixed to the familiar scene below, Vukovich's mind wandered. Perhaps because he was in a musty-smelling church, he thought of his wedding day nine years ago. Every Yugoslav in Fontana had shown up to see him take the hand of Patti Maravich, the Fontana Junior College Homecoming Queen. He'd worn his army uniform during the ceremony and left for Vietnam six days later. Patti had sobbed at the airport when he left; sobbed just like she always had during their frequent quarrels. They'd divorced about a year ago.

A well-dressed young man and woman staggered drunkenly past the law office to the entrance to the apartment house, oblivious to the rain. For something to do, Vukovich reached for the binoculars and watched the couple as they stood at the door, embraced and kissed. They parted briefly for what looked like an intense conversation. The man stuck his hand up the woman's dress; she pushed his hand away. More conversation. Finally, the woman opened her purse and removed a key. She unlocked the front door and they staggered inside.

He set the binoculars down. It seemed like it had rained the whole eighteen months he had been in Vietnam. During his first patrol a black sergeant had taught him how to keep a cigarette lit in the rain. "Leave it be," he'd said. "Just puff. Even if it's wet, it'll still smoke. But don't touch it or it'll fall apart." The method had worked well. He wondered how many cartons of cigarettes he'd smoked while he was there . . . fifty? Seventy?

Out of boredom, Vukovich picked up the small tape recorder, unwound the tape and played it from the beginning. *"Surveillance log begins—0700 hours . . . U.S. Treasury Field Force; Los Angeles . . . Law Office of Attorney Max Waxman, corner of Wilshire and Canberra Street. This is day three. The date is March thirteenth, time 0820 hours: Secretary May Shields arrives in her own vehicle and enters building. 0916 hours: Waxman arrives in his Cadillac and enters. 1003 hours: Latin male, approximately forty-five years arrives in blue Chevrolet bearing California license CLA609 and enters through front door. 1049 hours: Latin male departs.* The rest of the tape had similar tedious entries: people, most of whom Vukovich thought looked like underworld types, coming and going from Max the Money Man's office. Mary Shields, Waxman's long-legged blonde secretary (he remembered that Waxman's intelligence file noted that Shields was a counterfeit money courier whom Max once defended) left at 6 P.M.

The tapes reached the end of the last entry. John Vukovich turned off the recorder and set it back on the floor next to his chair. He stood up and stretched.

Suddenly, the door of the study flew open.

Richard Chance, a clean-featured, muscular man who, like Vukovich, was in his early thirties, stood in the well-lit hallway wearing a priest's robe. He raised his hands in benediction. *"Hocus pocus dominocus,"* he chanted. *"This is the message of the master.* How do I look, partner?"

"Like a T-man dressed up as a priest."

"Fuck you too," Chance said. He closed the door behind him and strode to the window. In the darkness, they both stared out the window without speaking. The rain glinted as it fell through the glow of street lights.

"I'd like to try parachuting out this window."

"Your chute wouldn't have time to open."

"Even when I was a kid I was into stunts. I used to crash my bicycle . . . jump off the roof of my house. Now I rarely miss a weekend of parachuting. I live for base-jumping.''

Vukovich gave a short laugh. ''Daredevil Dick,'' he said.

''I'm gonna parachute off the Vincent-Thomas Bridge in the next few weeks.''

''As an ex-paratrooper, I wish you luck.''

''Why don't you make the jump with me? I've got an extra chute.''

''No way,'' Vukovich said.

Richard Chance unzipped the priest's garb and took it off, tossed it onto a desk. He wore a white T-shirt, Levis, his gun and handcuffs. ''Ever go to church when you were a kid?'' he said.

''Every Sunday.''

''Did you believe any of it?''

''How do you mean?''

''Like do you believe that Jonah was actually swallowed by a whale?''

John Vukovich shrugged.

''All kidding aside . . . do you actually believe that some sum-bitch was, in actual fact, *swallowed by a whale?*''

Without waiting for an answer, Chance dropped to the floor and did push-ups in rapid succession.

John Vukovich kept his eyes on Waxman's office.

Finally Chance stopped and got to his feet. ''I wonder why they assigned us to work together?'' he said between deep breaths. ''Like why *us*?''

''All I know is that suddenly your name was next to mine on the Field Office duty board last month,'' Vukovich said, rubbing his eyes. ''Your guess is as good as mine.''

''I still haven't figured out where you're coming from.''

''Where I'm *coming* from?'' Vukovich said stoically. ''My father was a cop. When I was a kid I wanted to grow a beard and be a Serbian Orthodox priest. I served three years in the army and five years on the police department before coming to this job. I haven't had a day off in two weeks and at this very moment I couldn't give a shit less about you, Max Waxman, or 'where I'm coming from.' And the answer to your question is no, I'm not a snitch for Bateman."

Ignoring his reply, Chance pumped out another set of pushups before he flopped onto his back.

"I wonder what he's doing in there?" Vukovich said. "I wonder what he's doing right at this very moment?"

Catlike, Chance came to his feet. "Maybe he's counting some stacks of those nice, tax-free phony greenbacks." Carefully, he positioned a chair in front of the window and sat down next to Vukovich. He leaned forward and rested his elbows on the windowsill.

Again they stared out into the street, waiting.

"It'll be worth it if we catch someone delivering Max a load of those fifties and hundreds he's been dealing," Vukovich said, to make conversation.

"Will it?" Chance said. "Will it be worth spending the next three or four hours writing an affidavit for a search warrant? Then taking the affidavit to the Field Office and waiting while it's typed? Then driving thirty miles out to the U.S. attorney's house so some twenty-three-year-old mush-head lawyer can correct the spelling? Then after having the warrant retyped, drive thirty miles to the other side of town so some political-hack U.S. magistrate can complain about being awakened in the middle of the night to sign the warrant? Then drive all the way back here, kick Max's door in and spend the next twelve or fourteen hours after he bails out writing reports and filling out evidence forms? Will it be worth it?"

"On the other hand we might end up with a million dollar package and the printer himself."

"I'd rather go down there right now, boot Max's door and put a gun to his head," Chance said. "Force the rotten prick to name his source, and while we're at it, everyone else he knows who's holding so much as one single phony bill.

Then go arrest every fucking one of them. That would really be something. *Gangbusters.*''

After a while John Vukovich left his perch at the window. He walked around the room a few times to stretch his legs. The rain seemed to diminish.

"Do you think Max scores from Rick Masters?" Vukovich said.

"Probably. Everybody else in this town gets their paper from Tricky Ricky. Hell, he's on a ten-year run."

"How does he do it?"

"Easy," Chance said. "He prints the money all by himself and lets only a few select people he trusts do the dirty work of selling it. He doesn't deal with strangers, talks only on pay phones, and has the best lawyers money can buy. As long as he stays like that, he's untouchable."

Chance did more push-ups and Vukovich returned to the window. A breeze, tepid and gusting, blew mist inside.

Chance took more deep breaths. He stood up. "They say I'm a wild man, a hot-dog. You've heard that, haven't you?"

"I don't pay much attention to office talk," Vukovich said, though he had. On the other hand, he knew Chance led the office in arrests.

"My problem is that I'd rather put people in jail than sit around the Field Office all day jacking my jaws about how much the federal cost-of-living pay raise is going to be," Chance said.

"So would I," Vukovich said. He rubbed his eyes for a while.

Chance sat down at the desk. He took his wallet out of his back pocket and removed a tiny address book, flipped through the pages. "Decision, decisions," he muttered.

"Whatsat?"

"If you had a choice between an ugly redhead who likes to talk dirty or a beautiful blonde who's a bum lay, which one would you choose?"

"Have to meet 'em first." He continued to stare out the window.

Chance dialed a number. "It's me," he said. "Did I wake you? Sorry . . . what makes you think that? Who says I'm horny? Maybe I just called to say hello . . . On a stakeout. I tried to call you and let you know I had to work . . . And *I* miss you. I really do. If I didn't why would I have called?. . . How about tonight after I get off? So maybe I am. Maybe I do want to come over and jump on your bones. I can't help myself. . . ." He laughed. "Gotta run, baby . . . seeya in an hour or so." He set the receiver down.

"What makes you think we'll get off in an hour?" Vukovich said.

"Just lining up a piece of ass in case we do."

The breeze blew more mist in the window. John Vukovich stood up, closed the window, stretched and sat down again.

Max Waxman stood at the all-brass sink in his spacious, wood-paneled, office bathroom. Next to the bathroom mirror was a red wall phone which he expected to ring at any moment. As a matter of fact, he thought, the goddamn telephone was ruling his life.

He used a tiny, gold-plated razor to carefully shave around a pencil-thin mustache, then wiped his face with a clean towel. Shirtless, he only wore custom-made tropical wool slacks (he preferred the pleated European look because it made his puffy waistline look trimmer) and alligator boots. Leaning close to the mirror he bared his teeth, examining the bright white caps that covered fifty-eight-year-old yellowed choppers. Though he was bald on top, he was proud of the fact that the semicircle of ear-length hair which hung limply to his collar was generally healthy and required ebony retouching no more than once a week.

The phone rang; he grabbed it off the wall.

"Answering your own phone now?" Ruthie said. Her voice was a whine.

"So my secretary doesn't work nights," he said.

"I have a customer I absolutely cannot keep on the line for much longer," she said. "I need some samples like now."

"I'm waiting for a call right this minute."

"Let me know the minute you hear anything," she whined.

"I'm doing everything I can." Waxman hung up abruptly.

He splashed on French cologne from a tiny flagon which he knew cost as much as his father used to spend on a suit of clothes while he was eking out an existence in a grimy sandwich shop. He put on a shirt and sport coat, then walked back into his plushly-carpeted private office. He noticed that the sound of the rain had stopped. On the walls were African wildlife scenes and, facing his teakwood desk, a shiny wall unit loaded with electronic gear. He stepped to a standing Diebold safe which sat behind the desk under the window. He deftly worked the numbers on the combination lock (Trudy's measurements), opened the door. A ledger rested on the bottom shelf. He took it out and relocked the safe, then sat down at his desk.

He flipped the pages of the ledger book. Using a ruler, he underlined some figures with a red pen.

The phone rang. It was Rick Masters.

"You're a hard man to get in touch with," Waxman said. "I've left messages all over town."

"Been extra busy."

"Do you have anything?"

"I'll call you on the other number."

Max Waxman hung up the phone, then grabbed a magazine from the reception area on his way out of the office. Holding the magazine over his head as a makeshift umbrella, he avoided the puddles on the way to the gas station on the corner. The station's pay-booth phone was ringing when he got there. He stepped inside the booth and picked up the receiver.

"What's up?" Masters said.

"I need some more paper. I've got a broad on the line who's hot to score."

"Who is she?"

"I defended her husband in a murder case years ago. Ruthie's no problem; no problem at all."

"Where's her husband now?" Masters said.

"On Death Row in San Quentin."

"How much did you charge him for that favor?"

"Very funny."

"How much does she want?"

"She wants to see samples."

"I have some sample hundreds," Masters said. "I just finished them over the weekend. They're beautiful. Very beautiful."

"How many numbers?"

"Thirty different serial numbers."

"Sounds great. Can I get them tonight?"

"I'll send Blanca over. I should have used her rather than Carmine for the last deal and we would have avoided all the problems."

"Frankly, I'm glad to hear you say that. Since Carmine got arrested, I've gotten the feeling that you've been avoiding me. You haven't been returning my calls like you used to."

"Everyone lays low after a bust," Masters said.

"What about Falcone? Where do you stand with him?"

"He ripped me off," Masters said. "He's a dead man."

"Can you get *to* him in the joint?"

"Easier there than on the outside."

"Who ratted him in the first place?"

"Somebody in Las Vegas," Masters said. "It was in the

court papers the T-men filed for his arraignment. Las Vegas is full of snitches.''

"I've always said this.''

"I was letting him do too much," Masters said. "But, as you know, I need the insulation. I'm a prize to the Feds. This is what I'm up against.''

"Are we straight?" Waxman said.

"Straight?''

"Are we straight on this Falcone thing?''

"If we weren't straight, if I thought you'd ripped me off for six hundred K, would I be sending more samples?''

"I guess not.''

"You sound like you still have the jitters," Masters said. "There's nothing to worry about. Carmine got popped. He ripped us off for a load of paper. Life goes on.''

"I guess you're right," Waxman said.

The phone clicked. Waxman set the receiver back on the hook. He stepped out of the phone booth. Using the soggy magazine as an umbrella again, he ran back toward his office, surveying the street as he went. There were no suspicious-looking cars parked anywhere in the area. At the door of his office he turned and glanced at the All Souls Catholic Church and the office building next to it. There were no lights on in either structure. He entered his office and locked the front door behind him.

From a closet in the reception area he removed a white, canvaslike bullet-proof vest from a hanger. He shrugged off his coat and shirt, then donned the vest and fastened its Velcro straps tightly around his torso. He dressed again and returned to his desk. If there was anything he'd learned, it was that one simply could not be too cautious when dealing with the scum-of-the-earth. On the other hand, he knew that patience with the scum-of-the-earth paid for his vacations in Cannes every year, the mortgages on his Malibu beachfront home which was once owned by Clark Gable, and his ski chalet in Heavenly Valley.

His hands were wet with perspiration. He snatched a tissue from a desk drawer and dried them, then wiped his brow before tossing the tissue in a wastebasket. He picked up the receiver and dialed home.

"I'll be home in a little while," he told Trudy. "I have some business to take care of with Rick Masters," he said, making sure he pronounced the name clearly.

"Do I know him?"

"No, but I'll be home in a little while."

"You sound funny," she said. "Is everything okay?"

"Of course."

"Sorry I asked."

"After I take care of my business with *Rick Masters*, I'll be home." He made kiss sounds into the phone before he hung up.

He glanced at his Rolex. It was time for the eleven o'clock news. He opened a drawer and pressed a remote-control switch. The television which faced him from its perch in the wall unit came on. The half-hour program concluded with a story about a veterinarian who had structured a plastic beak for an injured duck. The handsome anchor man made happy talk about the story with the blonde anchor woman. Max Waxman wondered if her tits were as firm and heavy as Trudy's.

Finally there was a knock on the front door. Waxman headed into the reception area. He checked the peephole. Blanca stood outside wearing a white raincoat tied at the waist with a belt and holding an umbrella. She looked nervous. He hurried to the coat closet, removed a snub-nosed revolver from the top shelf and stuffed it into his coat pocket. He checked the peephole once again to make sure she was alone and unlocked the door. "Long time no see," he said, remembering her dancing naked on stage. "Do you have something for me?" She stepped in and closed her umbrella. Waxman reached around to lock the door behind her.

She smiled broadly. "In exchange for a drink."

"Of course," Waxman said. Having checked the peep-hole again, he motioned her into his office. As he opened a liquor cabinet, she sat down on the sofa.

"Bourbon?" he said.

"Fine." She glanced around the room.

Waxman brought the drinks over to her. "When do I get to see you on stage again?" he said in a friendly tone.

"Rick won't let me do it no more."

"That's a good reason," he said.

She removed an envelope from her purse and handed it to him. He opened it and pulled out a thin stack of fifty and one hundred dollar bills. He returned to his desk, held some of the bills up to a desk lamp. "High quality stuff," he said. "Very high quality. I know Rick had some doubts about me on this Falcone thing. I hope that's all over."

"Rick never says much to me about business. He told me to tell you that if you like the paper, he wants your order placed within the next day or two."

"That should be no problem."

"How's Trudy?" she said in an attempt to make conversation.

"Fine, just fine." He watched her for a moment as she sipped the drink. "You seem a little nervous."

"I'm always scared to death when I go somewhere with that stuff on me." She motioned to the counterfeit money.

"Understandable," he said.

She threw back the rest of her drink and stood up. "I'd better go. It's late."

"Stick around here and I'll have a thing for you to *do*," he said in a jocular manner.

She smiled and pinched him on the cheek on her way to the door.

He checked the peephole; the street was clear. He un-locked the door and opened it. Blanca stepped outside and opened her umbrella. "Talk that guy into letting you go back to Bodies Unlimited,'' Max Waxman said. ''I miss that tassel twirl.''

She smiled and waved as she headed toward the parking lot. Waxman closed and locked the door.

''I wonder who she is?'' Chance said as he leaned close to the window.

Vukovich used the binoculars. ''Never seen her before.''

In the parking lot, the woman climbed into a black Porsche. She drove out of the lot and headed east on Wilshire Boulevard. Vukovich dictated the license number of the car into the machine before he forgot it.

Rick Masters sat at the table nearest the door in the busy coffee shop. Through a rain-smeared window he watched Blanca park the Porsche in front of the place. She climbed out of the car and hurried inside. He waved and she joined him at the table. He noticed that her hands were shaking as she lit a cigarette. ''Well?'' he said.

''He's alone.''

''Where was he sitting?''

''At his desk . . . paper spread all over it.''

''I want you to think carefully before you answer this,'' he said. ''The curtain behind his desk . . . was it open or closed?''

''It was open a little bit.''

''How much is a little bit?''

''About a foot.''

He held out his hand. ''Let me have the keys to the Porsche.''

She handed them to him, puzzled. ''I'm leaving,'' he said. ''You take a taxi back to the pad.''

''Be careful, baby,'' she said as he left the table.

* * *

The television was still on.

Max Waxman finished making notations in his ledger. He sat back and rubbed his eyes for a moment. The phone rang.

"What do you think of the product?" Rick Masters said.

"I like it."

"When do you think you'll have an order for me?"

"Hell, I've just had the samples for a few minutes. Where are you calling from?"

"I'm in a pay booth," Masters said. "Uh, can you hold the line for a minute?"

"Sure," Waxman said. There was the sound of what could have been the receiver being set down on something . . . a car door slamming. An engine starting up. A car driving off.

As he became impatient waiting for Masters to return to the phone, Max Waxman heard the sound of a car driving slowly through the alley outside the window behind him. The car stopped. A car door opened and closed. Waxman sat quietly. Using the remote control device, he turned off the TV. He heard footsteps in the alley.

Suddenly window glass crashed. He spun around. The black barrel of a shotgun protruded through the smashed window. A deafening explosion. When he opened his eyes he was lying on his side in front of his desk and there was carbide smoke in the air. As he struggled to catch his breath and get into the safety of the reception area he realized that blood was surging from his neck. "Help me," he said as he tried to plug the warm leak with his hand. Crawling, he finally made his way into the reception area. Using all the strength he could muster, he got to his knees. He lunged forward, pulling the telephone off the receptionist's desk. A tight rivulet of blood squirted from his neck as he dialed O.

"Operator," a woman said. She sounded like Trudy.

"Help me," he said. "My law office is on the corner of Wilshire and Canberra and I've been shot." Suddenly he felt light-headed; light-headed and freezing cold.

"What is your name, sir?"

"Waxman." His voice sounded as if he was speaking from the end of a tunnel. A tunnel of dark red ice.

"What number are you calling from?" she said.

Waxman tried to recite the number from memory but couldn't. Slipping backward in the ice tunnel, he struggled to read the number off the phone, but it was covered with blood. For a moment he considered taking out a silk handkerchief which he knew was in his pocket and wiping the blood off the dial so he could read the number. Instead he just curled up tightly in a ball.

His last thought was that the bulletproof vest hadn't done him any good.

CHAPTER THREE

As cars of all descriptions drove by on the rain-swept Wilshire Boulevard, Vukovich pictured them parking in front of Max Waxman's office. He did this out of sheer boredom.

Chance was on the phone, making notes as he talked. "Thanks for the help," he said. He set the receiver down. "The black Porsche is registered to Reginald Musgrave in care of Father Donegan Television Productions. The legal owner is Paramount Studios."

"Father Donegan himself. The private eye priest."

"This broad I know is in love with him," Chance said.

"Huh?"

"She's in love with Father Donegan. She says he's the best-looking man she's ever laid eyes on."

"Sounds like she has a father complex," Vukovich said.

"I told her if old Father Donegan is like the rest of the movie crowd, he's probably married to his altar boy."

They laughed.

Suddenly a black-and-white police car with a flashing red light raced around the corner and pulled up in front of Waxman's office. A uniformed officer climbed out the driver's side holding a night stick. On the way to the front door of Waxman's office he dropped the night stick into a ring on his belt.

"What the hell is going on?" Chance said as he peered out the window.

Using a flashlight to illuminate the door of the office, the policeman knocked.

"Damn!" Vukovich said.

"The whole caper is blown," Chance said. "Three days down the drain. I can't believe it. I really can't believe this is happening."

No one came to the door.

After waiting a few minutes the officer walked over to the curtained bay window of the law office. He leaned down and peeked into the reception area through the space where the blinds met. He ran back to the front door, pulled his gun, then stepped back. With two powerful kicks (on the second kick, his hat fell off), he knocked the door off its hinges. Cautiously, the policeman stepped into the office.

Vukovich and Chance ran out of the study, down a flight of stairs and through a hallway past the open doors of the sanctuary. They ran out of the main door of the church and across the wet street. As they reached the front door of the law office, the young, blond-haired policeman trotted out.

Chance flashed his badge. "Treasury agents," he said. "Need any help?"

The officer kept his hand on the butt of his holstered revolver as he shined his flashlight on their badges. Without saying anything, he rushed over to the police car, reached in the driver's window and grabbed a microphone. "Three David thirteen requesting a homicide detective and a supervisor to Wilshire and Canberra," the officer said. "I've got a D.B. one eight seven."

In a bored tone, a female voice said roger. The officer

tossed the microphone back in the car. "What are you people doing here?" he said.

"We've had this place under surveillance for three days," Richard Chance said.

The policeman's glance alternated between the agents. He smiled wryly. "The surveillance is over, gents," he said. "There's a dead body inside."

"A bald guy with long hair just on the sides?" Vukovich asked.

"That's him," said the cop. "Why were you set up on him?"

"He's a counterfeit money dealer," Chance said.

"Looks like somebody let him have it through the rear window," the policeman said on his way to the trunk of the black-and-white. He unlocked the trunk and pulled out a coil of yellow rope, then slammed the trunk shut. "Would you mind securing the front door for me? I need to rope off the alley in back."

Vukovich nodded. The policeman hurried through the parking lot toward the rear of the building.

Cautiously, Vukovich followed Chance through the front doorway. The reception area was neat: blue shag carpeting, cartoon caricatures of lawyers and judges on the walls.

Max Waxman's body was in the fetal position on the floor next to the reception desk. His right hand gripped a telephone receiver which, along with desk litter, looked like it had been yanked off the desk. The back of his tweed coat and the front of his green silk shirt were soaked with blood, as was the carpeting around his body. A trail of blood extended from inside his office. For some reason, Vukovich thought of snail tracks. Max Waxman's red snail tracks.

Chance stepped into the inner office.

"We'd better get the hell out of here," Vukovich said. "This is a crime scene."

Chance ignored the warning and continued into the office. Vukovich followed, hesitating at the door. The red trail extended from the reception room back to a blood-splattered desk.

Behind the desk was a widely barred window which faced an alley leading from the parking lot. The window was broken and glass was scattered on top of a safe and on the floor in front of the window. On Waxman's desk was a gray ledger.

"Shotgun through the window," Chance whispered as he stepped to the other side of the desk. Vukovich heard the policeman tromping around outside in the alley.

"We were watching this place and he was dead," Vukovich said. His eyes were riveted on the blood trail.

A breeze came in through the front door, and pushed it fully open. With the wind came the smell of death from the soaked carpet. Vukovich turned and headed for the door.

Outside, the rain had diminished to a drizzle.

A police car with swirling red lights rounded the corner and splashed to a halt in front of the office. An overweight, uniformed sergeant with slicked-back hair took his time climbing out of the car. He held a metal clipboard.

The blond cop trotted to the sidewalk from the alley. He spoke with the sergeant and pointed at Vukovich.

"Feds?" the sergeant said as if the word denoted leprosy.

Vukovich approached the sergeant. "We were staked out . . ."

"The victim is a funny money dealer," the young officer interrupted. "These people were staked out on him."

"People?" the sergeant said.

The young officer pointed at Chance, who stood in the office doorway. The sergeant nodded.

"I asked them to watch the front while I roped off the alley in back," he said. "The shots look like they came from the back window."

The sergeant grunted and made notes on a clipboard.

A few moments later a tall, sleepy-eyed homicide detective wearing an out-of-shape brown polyester sport coat arrived. The young officer repeated the information and he made notes on *his* metal clipboard.

Chance said something about having left his cigarettes at the church, then jogged across the street.

Vukovich lolled about on the sidewalk, watching as police fingerprint and photo men arrived and wandered into the law office. Chance returned. Standing next to a police car, he lit a cigarette.

Flashbulbs popped; cars came and left. The homicide detective made a phone call from the pay phone at the service station. A few minutes later a lieutenant arrived. Then later, a captain. More briefings.

Finally the homicide detective ambled out of the law office and approached the T-men. "I'm Ed Lindberg," he said.

The partners introduced themselves.

"Any guesses as to who would want to dump this guy?" Lindberg said as he rearranged pages on his clipboard.

"He's a dealer," Chance said. "Dealers have enemies."

"No shit," he said sarcastically.

"A woman stopped by about an hour ago," Vukovich said. "She was driving a Porsche that registers to Paramount Studios."

"License plate?"

"XJR seven one four," Chance said. "Think she could be good for the murder?"

The detective noted the plate number on the clipboard. He shook his head. "If she left an hour before the first police car arrived, she's not good for the murder. The victim phoned the police emergency number while he was dying and it looks like he was shotgunned from the alley in the rear."

"What did she look like?" Lindberg said.

"Mexican, thirty, about five foot four, one fifteen, long black hair, a real good lookin' bitch," Chance said. "She wore a white raincoat and carried an umbrella."

"I'll need a copy of your surveillance log sometime tomorrow," Lindberg said as he dug a business card out of his suit pocket. He handed it to Vukovich.

"Sure," Chance said. He handed the detective a Treasury business card. Lindberg shoved it in his shirt pocket and headed back into the law office.

Vukovich returned to the church study and gathered up the equipment as Chance went for the government car. As Vukovich left the church by a rear door, Chance was waiting. He opened the passenger door and climbed into the sedan. Chance drove out of the church parking lot and onto Wilshire Boulevard, past the squadron of police cars parked in front of Max Waxman's office.

Suddenly, Chance reached under the seat. He pulled out the ledger book which had been on Waxman's desk.

"Jesus," Vukovich said. "Is that the . . . ?"

"You guessed it, partner," Chance said.

Chance pulled to the curb in front of a Mexican restaurant. He proudly handed the ledger book over to Vukovich.

After flicking on the car's dome light Vukovich leafed through the book. The pages listed the names and phone numbers of buyers and the amounts of counterfeit money purchased. Some of the names were of people Vukovich had arrested in the past.

Chance pointed to a page near the back of the book, snapped the page open with a finger. On it was a list of delivery dates and amounts with Rick Masters written at the top of the page. "Max's source was Masters. This proves it."

"Why the hell would a lawyer keep *records* of his distribution network? This book could have put him in the joint for twenty years."

"He had so much business there probably was no other way to keep everything straight. He was peddling funny money and dope hot and heavy over a long period of time and probably just felt secure."

Vukovich flipped more pages. "Incredible," he said.

"With Max gone, we're a step closer to putting Rick Masters out of business once and for all. Max was his main man."

Vukovich swallowed twice. "That was a crime scene and this book is evidence," he said. "What if the cop realizes the book is missing?" He handed it back to Chance.

"He wasn't there long enough to be able to remember everything that was on the desk. Besides, he never saw us go inside."

"You shouldn't have done it," Vukovich said.

Chance stared at him for a moment. "What are you trying to tell me, partner?" he said.

Vukovich stared at a dark and deserted Wilshire Boulevard. A beat-up Chevy filled with Latin men rounded a corner, ground gears on its way up the street. He didn't answer.

"If you feel that strongly about it, I'll just turn the car around and go back right now," Chance said. "Just say the word."

"I didn't say that," Vukovich said, still staring ahead.

"Are you saying you won't carry part of the weight if anything does happen? I have a right to know."

Vukovich met Chance's stare. "We could both get fired for this little trick. If you expect me to take heat you should have asked me before you did it."

"I apologize," Chance said. "I should've tuned you in before hand. I'm serious about going back to face the music. Just say the word."

"Don't ever pull anything like that again when you're with me unless you ask." The sound of mariachi music came from the Mexican restaurant.

"If I would have asked, what would you have said?"

"I'd have said that the cops would have probably let us make a copy of the book after it was booked into evidence."

Richard Chance was conciliatory. "It was sort of a stupid risk to take," he admitted.

"I'm no snitch," Vukovich said finally.

"Funny, maybe that's why I grabbed the book. I wouldn't have done it if I was with someone I didn't trust."

Chance checked the rearview mirror. He pulled back into traffic and continued to head toward downtown. Steering into the left lane, he turned onto Alvarado and passed neon bar signs with names like the Owl Tree Inn, the Place and the Circus. Across the street was MacArthur Park. There, like so many pieces in a surreal parlor game, drunk vagrants and trolling queers wandered about in the greenish light of mercury-vapor street lamps.

Chance laughed. "Max the Money Man left us something in his will," he said, stopping to catch his breath. Finally, Vukovich joined in the laughter.

At Temple Street Chance turned right and headed to the Field Office, where they locked up the surveillance equipment and completed the daily log.

As he left the Federal Building alone that night, Vukovich rolled the window down to avoid falling asleep at the wheel. With the cool air blowing on his face, he thought again of finding Waxman's body curled up on the floor, unable to shake the image from his mind. After ten years of police work, he knew it was a normal reaction to a death scene. He'd get over it.

CHAPTER FOUR

Vukovich steered off the Pasadena Freeway and drove east on Colorado Boulevard through the suburban Highland Park business area. At the bottom of a slight grade, he swerved into an enormous shopping mall parking lot which, because of the hour, was almost empty. In the corner of the parking lot was a large log cabin-style building. The roof and eaves had been cleverly plastered and painted to give it a snow-covered effect, and a wooden sign in front read Yukon Territory—Steaks and Seafood. There were fifty or so cars parked in front of the place.

Inside, the walls were ornamented with snowshoes, fur pelts and Winchester rifles. Vukovich headed straight for the bar. It was half-filled, a business crowd. He sat at a bar stool next to the waitress station. Patti was serving drinks to a group seated in a corner booth. She was dressed in a red gay-nineties costume with a short puffy skirt and black lace stockings. She had long legs, flowing black hair, a healthy bustline and, like all the Maravich women, a near-perfect complexion that was clear and smooth. Carrying an empty tray, she came to the bar.

"I had a feeling you'd be in tonight," she said as she counted change.

"Why?" he said as he lit a cigarette.

"Maybe it's because you haven't stopped by in such a long time. So how've you been?" Her tone was casual.

"Fine."

"How's your mother getting along?"

"She's staying with my aunt and uncle because she hasn't been feeling well lately. The doctor has her scheduled for some tests."

"How's your new partner?"

"He's okay."

"I thought you said that he's a crazy man; that no one in the Field Office wanted to work with him," she said.

"He's different all right. But he's a hard worker and a good cop."

"Wouldn't you rather work with Hart? You always liked him."

"Yeah, but my beloved agent-in-charge just came back from a management seminar. The new rule is that older agents aren't supposed to work with the younger ones: something about bad habits rubbing off."

"Bad habits like coming home at night rather than working lots of unpaid overtime?"

"That's part of the job."

"Something's bothering you," she said. "You have that look in your eyes."

He shrugged.

"And that was exactly the way you'd answer me when we were married. Big case?"

"Surveillance. I'm just tired."

"Sure," she said scornfully.

A tall, athletic-looking bartender with kinky blond hair stepped to the bar station. He said hello to Vukovich and served him a drink, then moved back to the other end of the bar.

"How's school going?" Vukovich asked as he sipped the drink.

"Great. I'll be teaching third graders by this time next year."

"Do you need anything?"

"Nice of you to ask," she said, avoiding eye contact. "But I'm doing just fine. The tips here are great."

They chatted at the bar as she carried drinks to tables for the next hour until the place finally closed.

As the bartender locked the front door, Patti sat with Vukovich at a cocktail table. She sipped a glass of wine. "I see things so much clearer now," she said.

He gave her a puzzled look.

"Our relationship. Our marriage."

"How so?"

"It goes back to when you volunteered for a second combat tour in Vietnam without telling me. There we were, separated for a year and I was so afraid that something was going to happen to you and then you stayed there rather than come home when you had the chance. I simply couldn't understand it."

"I didn't think you knew I'd volunteered to stay."

"I knew," she said.

Vukovich drank silently. For a moment he wondered why the hell he'd come to see her.

"I think I understand your family better now, too," she said. "I'd never been around policemen in my whole life. The first time I heard all you men sitting around on a Sunday afternoon talking police talk, I didn't know what to think. All that talk about shootings and choking people out and how rotten the blacks are absolutely turned me off. My father was an English teacher. I'd never heard talk like that before."

"It's just the way cops are."

"I understand that now. I really do. Policemen are drawn to violence. God knows why, but they're drawn to the underside of life. It's just the way they are . . . like people who work at a morgue. I'm sure they have some reason for wanting to work there as opposed to somewhere else.''

"How are your folks?'' Vukovich said in an attempt to change the subject.

"They're fine,'' she said laconically. "May I ask you something I never had the courage to ask you when we were married?''

He nodded.

"Just why *did* you choose to stay in Vietnam rather than come home to me, to someone who loved you? Why?''

Vukovich didn't answer her immediately . . . how could he explain it?

"I guess I was just caught up in it all,'' he said after a long pause.

"What does that mean?''

"You'd never understand.''

"Please,'' she said. "I'll accept whatever you say. I want to understand.''

He finished his drink and looked her in the eye. "Would you understand if I told you that I stayed there so I could kill more of them? That I hated 'em that much? Is that what you wanted to hear ten years ago? Did you want to hear about the time we set off a claymore mine and blew the legs off thirteen gooks at once? We called it the Duc Loc Dance Contest. Is that what you wanted to hear?''

"I never forgave you for not coming home when you had the chance. I think that's when our problems really started.''

"I guess I shouldn't have lied to you about it.''

"Nothing's changed,'' she said. "You still would rather make war than make love. You're like all the men in your family. You're like all cops. I feel sorry for you.''

John Vukovich pushed his chair back and stood up. "Gotta run,'' he said coldly.

"I'm sorry I brought it up again,'' she said loudly as he walked toward the door.

* * *

The apartment house Vukovich lived in (he and Patti had sold the condo during the divorce) was of the typical two-story, stucco, ten-units-surrounding-a-pool variety which blanketed L.A. His apartment was on the ground floor. In the kitchen he grabbed cheese and lunch meat from the refrigerator and, standing over the sink, snacked for a while.

Realizing he was too keyed-up to fall asleep he stretched out on the living room sofa and read the newspaper, finishing with a detailed story about restaurant robbers who'd beaten their victims and forced them to perform sex acts. He tossed the newspaper down, stood up and stretched.

On the mantel over a simulated fireplace was an old photograph of him and his father at his Uncle Branko's winery in Fontana. His father, like the other Vukovich men, was a square-shouldered man with rough hands and short legs. Some said the men in the family simply *looked* like policemen.

Staring at the photo, he recalled his father's advice when he first became a cop. "Nobody likes a stool pigeon," he had said. Over the years, Vukovich had come to realize that the advice was the essence of police wisdom: cultivate informants . . . but never, *never* be one.

After an unsuccessful attempt to get interested in the late show he turned off the television and crawled into bed. The windows were open and he could hear rain dripping from the eaves onto the driveway. He woke once during the night because of the nightmare he had over and over again: Vietnam. It had been a sweltering, humid day. The villager had pointed the way to an arms cache. As always in the dream, the members of patrol argued bitterly. Some believed the villager. Others didn't. Fearing land mines and booby traps, Vukovich made the villager walk a few feet in front of him as the rest of the patrol followed. The trail led along the edge of a rice paddy and into some trees. There was nothing but the sound of boots tromping mud.

Then, the explosion and the sound of helicopter blades rippling the rice paddy waters, and the medics huddled over him digging into his guts with rubber-gloved hands.

Sleepily, he ran his hand across his scarred abdomen. He rolled over and went back to sleep.

When he awoke his first thought was of Max Waxman's book.

CHAPTER FIVE

The bullpen was a large room in the Field Office which was crammed with rows of gray metal desks facing one another. On the walls were link analysis charts, blow-ups of counterfeit notes and black-and-white surveillance photos of people standing near automobiles or coming and going from houses.

Hart had spent most of the day there writing useless status reports on some old counterfeiting cases. The pat phrase was: *There are no new investigative leads in this case since the date of the last report.* This particular required-by-the-Manual-of-Operation task bothered him as much as it did almost thirty years ago when he came on the job. His desk was in the corner and was shielded by a a partition on which were pinned photographs of paper pushers of various types: passers who were rumored to be in town, fugitives, active counterfeiters. Prominent among the photos was a booking shot of a nattily dressed Rick Masters, whom he'd arrested three times in the past ten years. All the arrests had been thrown out of federal court for one technical reason or another. Next to Masters's mug shot was a government-issued calendar with most of the days in January marked off. The intercom box on his desk buzzed. ''Just a reminder that your status reports are two days overdue,'' Agent-in-Charge Bateman said in his usual irritated-but-under-control tone.

''Thanks,'' Hart said. The intercom clicked off. Angrily he locked his desk and left the office. He checked a government sedan out from the basement federal motor pool and drove at a leisurely pace through downtown L.A. to the freeway. The trip to Griffith Park took less than fifteen minutes. There, he took a winding uphill road past an ancient merry-go-round. At the end of the paved road he continued on in the dirt until he made his way to a small clearing. He parked the government sedan on the crest of a hill which provided a view of the exclusive Los Feliz residential area and East Hollywood. He removed a small pocket calendar and a pen from his coat pocket and marked off today's date which, if he'd figured correctly, made it two months and three days to go until retirement.

Hart glanced at himself in the rearview mirror. Now that his hair had turned gray, he looked more like a banker or an insurance salesman than a federal cop. Come to think of it, maybe he would have been better off as a banker . . . at least he would have made more money and spent more time at home with his family.

Hart leaned over and adjusted the volume switch on the Field Office radio to high, then climbed out of the car. He took off his suit coat and draped it across the seat. Next he removed a folding chair and a couple of *Field and Stream* magazines from the trunk. After setting up the chair to face the view, he loosened his necktie and sat down to read. At dusk he heard Bateman call him on the air. He stepped to the car and reached in for the microphone. ''Go ahead.''

''What is your current location?''

''In the valley.''

''That's a roger,'' the sneaky Bateman said, having made

sure he was still on the air and hadn't gone home early.

Hart replaced the chair and magazines in the trunk, then drove toward his Burbank apartment. He considered having dinner at an Italian restaurant on Riverside Drive, but decided against it because it was a place he and his wife, who had died a year earlier, had frequented. Instead he opted for a chiliburger and fries at a fast food stand near his place. He spent the evening alone in his apartment, reading a couple of chapters in a fly-fishing book. The shot of whisky he drank before climbing into bed failed to bring sleep. He couldn't stop thinking about the way his wife used to chat with him at the dinner table in her unassuming way about the events of her day.

He climbed out of bed and switched on the television set, which rested on a chest of drawers next to two framed photographs. One was a color shot of his look-alike, auburn-haired wife and daughter standing next to him in front of the Lake Tahoe cabin where they'd spent more vacations than he could remember; the other was a family portrait of his daughter, son-in-law and two-year-old grandson who now lived in Washington, D.C. Because he'd put everything in storage after moving from the old house after his wife's death, the photos and a few kitchen gadgets were the only tangible things left to remind him of twenty-five years of marriage.

There was a knock at his door. Hart got out of bed and trudged through the living room. He was bare chested, only wearing pajama bottoms. "Who's there?" he called through the door.

"Someone's broken into my apartment. The door of my apartment appears to have been tampered with. I'm afraid to go in."

Hart peeked out the window. A woman dressed in a brown business suit and holding a briefcase stood outside.

She had short hair sprinkled with gray; appeared to be in her forties. He opened the door.

"I'm sorry to bother you," she said with fear in her voice. "When I moved in yesterday, the manager mentioned to me that you were a policeman."

Hart hurried back to the bedroom, grabbed his gun and returned to the living room. "Does anyone else have access to your apartment?" he said as he headed out the door. He motioned her back when she tried to follow.

"I live alone," the woman said.

There were pry marks on her door. Standing to the side he pushed the door open, then reached in and turned on the light.

He cautiously stepped through the doorway. Drawers were upturned in the kitchen area. Gun first, he moved to the bedroom. More opened drawers. After checking the closets and the bathroom, he returned to the hallway. "I'm afraid you've been burglarized," he said.

"I just moved in yesterday," she said incredulously. "I just moved in."

He noticed that her hands were shaking.

"It's better not to touch anything in there," he said. "You can call the police from my apartment." As he ushered her back inside he realized he wasn't fully dressed and felt a tinge of embarrassment; he quickly excused himself and threw on a shirt and trousers. As he stepped back into the living room, he noticed that the woman remained standing near the door. She held her briefcase in front of her in a manner of a self-conscious sales person.

Hart took the briefcase from her. "Please sit down," he said. "I'll make coffee."

"No, thank you."

"Are you sure?" he said as he went to the phone and dialed the police.

"I've never had anything like this happen to me," she said as he completed the call.

"Please sit down," he said. "The police will be here in a few minutes."

"I prefer to stand, thank you."

"What's in the briefcase?" he said, trying to put the woman at ease. "It's pretty heavy to lug around, isn't it?"

"Books," she said. "I teach at U.C.L.A."

"I know you feel terrible right about now," he said, "but I think it would help if you would just sit down and relax for a few minutes. Everything is going to be okay."

"I'm Donna Fields."

"Jim Hart."

"Thank you for your help, Mr. Hart, but I think I'll go back to my apartment and wait for the police. This is something I should be able to handle myself."

As she spoke Hart noticed her clear blue eyes, her attractive figure. He guessed that she was athletically inclined, probably belonged to a health club like everyone else in L.A. Like his wife, she wore only a hint of makeup.

"If there's anything I can do, please let me know," he said as she walked out the door. After locking up the apartment again Hart went back to bed. Now fully awake, he thumbed through the fly-fishing book again to try to make himself sleepy. Finally, he turned out the light and closed his eyes.

Another light knock on the door. Hart dressed quickly and hurried into the living room, checked the peephole. It was Donna Fields. He flicked the light switch. As he opened the door, she covered her face and broke into tears. "I'm afraid to be there alone," she cried. "I'm afraid they'll come back."

He hustled her into the apartment and shut the door. "I've just moved to L.A. and I don't know anyone," she said as he ushered her into a seat at his kitchen table. "They took everything I own. Everything."

Hart put water on for coffee and turned the rest of the

lights on in the apartment. "What you're feeling is very normal," he said as he handed her a box of tissues. She took one and wiped her eyes.

"I've read about the victim syndrome," she said. "But I never thought I'd be one."

Hart prepared instant coffee.

"You're safe now," he said as he set the cup and saucer in front of her.

"Why did they pick *my* apartment?" she said.

"Probably just the luck of the draw."

"Do you think they were watching me?"

"They probably just knocked on your door. No one was home, so they just broke in."

"The thought of someone having been inside my apartment gives me the creeps. I don't even think I can live there now. I feel as if I've been raped . . . violated."

She sipped coffee and wiped her eyes again. "I feel so foolish bothering you again," she said, standing to leave. "I'm going to a motel until I can find another apartment." Her jaw dropped. "But I can't. They stole my money . . . my credit cards."

"You're staying here tonight," Hart said.

"I can't do that."

"The sofa makes into a very comfortable bed. You're staying here." He went to a hall closet, brought back bedding and set it on the sofa.

"Please don't treat me like the average helpless female."

"I'm treating you like a neighbor," Hart told her firmly. After she finished her coffee Hart retreated to his bedroom and spent a restless night, unable to forget the woman sleeping just outside his room on the sofa.

"I feel completely foolish about the way I acted last night," Donna Fields said as they sat at his kitchen table the next morning. "What happened last night is indicative of

American culture. The burglary was caused by economic injustice and my inability to deal with it properly was caused by my subconscious acceptance of the subjugated female role.''

"I guess that's one way of looking at it.''

"I acted like the typical female . . . you like the typical man, and the burglar reacted typically to his environment. I'm sure he couldn't change his behavior any more than we could.''

"I once knew a burglar who was shot while committing a burglary. He recovered in a prison hospital and never committed another burglary again. The prison psychiatrist called it 'bullet therapy'.''

"How did he earn a living when he was released?''

"He became a car thief.'' He smiled wryly.

Donna Fields wrinkled her brow in disapproval at the remark. "Have you ever been married?'' she asked. She had a self-conscious edge to her voice.

Hart didn't answer immediately. "My wife . . . uh . . . passed away about a year ago,'' he said. *Why couldn't he say it without choking up?*

"I'm sorry.''

"And you?'' He cleared his throat.

"I'm divorced. It's been almost two years. I've made the transition. I was married for fifteen years, but I've made the transition.''

"I bet it wasn't easy. I mean, fifteen years is a long time to have been married.''

"When I was married I spent my whole life worrying about my husband . . . what he would think about this or that. Now I have no one to answer to but myself and I'm quite pleased. I can get up in the middle of the night and pop popcorn if I want to. In a certain way I guess I've come to enjoy the selfishness.''

Hart sipped his coffee. "I think I'm still in the transition stage.''

"The first few months are the worst. My social life was based around married couples my husband and I socialized with. Of course they just stopped calling. My husband is a professor at U.C. Berkeley and my life was based around his. But after a while I just stopped being lonely. Now I enjoy not having to answer to anybody. I have my own career. And in my free time, I do precisely what I want to. One can derive a certain satisfaction in the freedom of being alone." She checked her wristwatch. "I must be going. I have an early class." She stood up. "Thanks again for everything," she said as she gathered up her things.

"Glad I could help." He walked to the door and opened it for her. As she left, the thought occurred to him that she was the first woman who'd been in the apartment since he'd moved in.

Before leaving for work Hart stared at the phone for a moment, considering whether or not to call his daughter just to chat; he decided against it and left for the office instead . . . he'd recently spoken to her and didn't want to seem like a pest.

Hart lifted a clipboard off a hook near the door, scribbled his name on the office sign-in sheet. He was the first one in.

The phone rang before he'd reached his desk.

"This is Detective Lindberg, L.A.P.D. Robbery-Homicide. Do you have an Agent Chance and an Agent Vukovich who work there?" he asked.

"Yes," Hart said.

"I'd like to speak to Tom Bateman, the agent-in-charge."

"He's not in yet," Hart said. "May I take a number?"

"Sure," Lindberg said.

"I'll have him call you," Hart said after taking down the number. He set the receiver down and dug an office roster out of his desk, looked through it for Vukovich's phone number.

He placed the call; Vukovich answered.

"Jim Hart here. Can you meet me at the Angel's Flight?" he said because he didn't trust the office phones.

"Is there a problem?" Vukovich asked.

There was a silence.

"I'll be there as soon as I can," Vukovich said. Both men hung up quickly.

CHAPTER SIX

The Angel's Flight, a cop's bar, was a small, run-down place located on Sunset Boulevard a few blocks from Dodger Stadium. Over its entrance was a winged neon rail car heading down what looked like a roller-coaster track. In order to provide a boozy atmosphere for those who drank there during the day, the place had no windows. Hart maneuvered his G-car into a parking space behind the bar and turned off the engine.

Vukovich arrived a few minutes later. He parked his car and climbed in the passenger seat of Hart's sedan. "What's up?" he said, impatiently.

"An L.A.P.D. detective named Lindberg phoned the office this morning," Hart said. "He mentioned you and Chance, and left a message for the boss."

"Damn."

Hart leaned forward against the steering wheel. He knew enough not to ask what the problem was. Only crooks were stupid enough to incriminate themselves.

"Did he say anything else?"

Hart shook his head.

Vukovich bit his lip. "Thanks for the tip-off," he said as he stared at nothing in particular.

"How do you like working with Chance?" Hart said.

Vukovich shrugged in response.

"I understand others have refused to work with him."

Vukovich nodded. "That's what I hear," he said.

"Have you ever been beefed before?"

"When I was on the police department a prisoner spit in my face. I was accused of punching him in the stomach so hard it knocked him out."

"Handcuffs on or off?"

"I took 'em off before I let him have it."

"Any witnesses?"

Vukovich shook his head. "My word against his."

"The ones where there are no witnesses are the easy ones," Hart said. "Watch out for Bateman. He likes in-house investigations. It's the way he gets his charge."

"A twisted son of a bitch."

Hart leaned back in the seat. "The least twisted person I've ever known in my whole life was a fellow that used to be my next-door neighbor," he said. "He came home from work every night at the same time, mowed his lawn every Saturday morning. He took his two-week vacation at the same place every year. Lighting the charcoal for a weekend barbecue was probably the most exciting part of his life."

Vukovich furrowed his brow as if to say *so what?*

Hart cleared his throat. "He once told me that if he had a choice, the last job, the very *last* job he would ever choose would be that of a cop . . . funny." Hart looked at his hands resting on the steering wheel, waiting.

"Bateman'll never get me to talk," Vukovich said.

"On the other hand, sometimes copping out on a small beef and taking a short suspension is better than ending up with a cloud over one's head. If you beat Bateman, he'll wait for you. He'll play catch-up."

"Sure," Vukovich said disdainfully. "Take a suspension and end all chances of ever being promoted."

"Come to think of it, I haven't taken a day's suspension in the almost thirty years I've been in this crazy outfit," Hart said as if he'd just had the realization.

"Are you telling me you've never broken the rules?"

"When I was your age I was in a jam or two. But looking back on it, I think I might have been trying too hard, taking things personal when I really shouldn't have."

"It must have been a lot easier to make cases then . . ." Vukovich said. "Less legal technicalities. . . ."

Hart nodded in agreement. "But on the other hand, it was easier for the crooks to bribe the judges. Times have changed, but not much."

"I'd better go call Chance," Vukovich said. He reached for the door handle.

"I want you to know that you can always come to me if you want to talk about things."

"Thanks," Vukovich mumbled as he climbed out of the car.

John Vukovich hurried into the bar. The pay phone was located in a rear hallway next to a restroom. The sound of country-and-western music and the conversation of raucous morning drinkers came from inside the bar. He dropped a dime and dialed Chance's home number. He answered, and Vukovich told him what he'd learned.

"I don't remember going inside Waxman's office . . . do you?" Chance said.

"What if the cop heard us inside when he was in the alley?"

"We can't help what *other* people heard. We only know what *we* heard. It's either that or we turn in the book, take a suspension and forget any chance of getting promoted."

"What if they find our fingerprints inside the office?"

"We didn't touch anything," Chance said.

"I'm on my way to the Field Office," Vukovich said after a short pause.

"Are we together on this thing?"

"I guess there's no other way to go."

On his way to the Field Office Vukovich had the urge to light a cigarette even though he didn't smoke.

Once there, he found a "see me" note bearing Bateman's initials on his desk. He tossed the note in a wastebasket and headed down the hall to Bateman's office. He took a deep breath and stepped into a reception area. Bateman's gray-haired secretary, a fiftyish, dissipated woman who invariably wore the same red dress, stopped typing when he walked in. "He has someone in there already," she told him, neither smiling nor frowning.

"Send him in," Bateman called from his office.

Vukovich stepped inside. An abundance of hanging plants and family pictures decorated the office; Vukovich recalled that Jim Hart had once told him Bateman patterned the accoutrements from an article about office decoration in *Government Executive* magazine.

Lindberg, the homicide detective, sat in a chair in front of Bateman's desk. He looked like he needed a shave. Bateman smiled, pointed to a chair. A tall man, he wore a long-sleeved, white shirt which everyone knew covered matching hula-girl forearm tattoos. Though only slightly overweight, his features nevertheless were puffy. His balding pate was covered by a thick bridge of black hair extending across his frontal lobe.

Vukovich sat down.

"I take it you've met Detective Lindberg?" Bateman said.

Vukovich nodded while the detective covered his mouth and yawned.

"Has anyone mentioned to you what this might be about?" Bateman said, fidgeting.

"No."

"Have you spoken with Jim Hart this morning?"

"No," Vukovich said without hesitation.

"I thought he might have given you some input," Bateman said. "He took the call from Detective Lindberg this morning."

"A call about what?"

"There's a book missing from Waxman's office," Lindberg said without making eye contact with Vukovich. "When the patrol officer first arrived at the scene he saw a book on Waxman's desk. He remembers because it was the only thing on the desk. The book wasn't there when I arrived. I thought that you or your partner might have picked it up. If you did, I want it back."

Vukovich didn't say anything. He stared at Bateman.

Bateman fidgeted. "This is no big thing," he said. "No one can fault an agent for trying a little too hard. If you have the book you can turn it over and we'll forget the whole thing; no big *impact*. In fact, no *impact* whatsoever."

"I didn't take any book."

"Did you go inside the office?" Bateman said.

"No."

"Did Chance go inside the office?"

"No."

"How do you totally know Chance didn't go inside the office?" Bateman said.

"We were together the whole time."

"That's viable," Bateman said after a pause.

The detective sat staring at his hands. Vukovich thought he looked embarrassed; angry, but embarrassed.

"I wouldn't care about the book if the murder looked solvable otherwise," Lindberg said. "But at this point it's a who-dunit. So I need the book."

Vukovich turned and looked the detective in the eye. "Like I said, I don't have any book."

"Did the uniformed officer ask you and Chance to watch

the front door while he roped off the alley?'' Bateman asked. He began to make notes on a yellow pad.

''Yes.''

''Well?''

''Well what?'' Vukovich said, trying to avoid sounding sarcastic.

''Did you watch the front door of the law office?'' Bateman said.

Detective Lindberg lit a cigarette, leaned forward to rest his elbows on his knees while he took a couple of deep drags.

''Yes, we did,'' Vukovich said.

''Did anyone try to enter while you were there?'' Bateman said.

''No.''

Lindberg glanced at his wristwatch. He straightened up in the chair, as if he were anxious to leave.

''So as far as you know, no one except the uniformed officer entered the law office, is that right?'' Bateman said.

''That's right.''

Bateman scribbled more notes. Probably, Vukovich reasoned, because he couldn't think of any other questions. Finally, he set the pen down and looked at Lindberg.

''Why were you watching Waxman's office last night?'' Lindberg asked. He picked tobacco off the end of his tongue.

''Waxman was involved in dealing counterfeit money,'' Vukovich said. ''We were trying to identify his source.''

''You had reason to believe that he was operating right out of his law office?'' Lindberg said.

''Right.''

Lindberg said he didn't have any other questions.

''Thank you for your input,'' Bateman said. ''You may go.''

Vukovich stood up. Without saying anything, he left the office. Chance was sitting on a sofa in the reception area.

Vukovich ignored him and returned to his desk. As he sat down, he realized that the middle of his back was wet with perspiration. He fiddled with papers for a while because he couldn't concentrate enough to write his overdue weekly activity report.

Other special agents, who wore either undercover clothing (lots of leather and suede jackets and Italian-cut trousers and shirts) or business attire (cheap dark suits and wing-tipped shoes) filtered into the room and sat down at desks. He could tell by the lack of conversation that, as always, the word of the in-house investigation had spread quickly.

Bateman stepped out of his office and motioned to Chance.

The agent followed him into the office and sat down. He exchanged nods with the detective.

Bateman closed a file folder on his desk and smiled. "Vukovich cleared up the matter of the book that is missing from Max Waxman's office," he said. "He said that you and he took it because you thought it might aid your investigation. No harm done. We just need your side of the story; your *input*. I'm sure you can relate to that."

The detective looked as if he'd suddenly developed a migraine headache. He closed his eyes and rubbed his temples.

"I don't know what you're talking about," Chance said.

"Are you saying that you totally weren't *at* Max Waxman's office last night?"

"No."

"So you admit being there?"

"Of course."

"And you admit being inside the office for some period of time?"

"We didn't go inside the office."

"That's funny," Bateman said. "Vukovich said you did. He said that you and he snatched a book off Waxman's desk."

"If he said that, he's a goddamn liar."

"I think you're making a mountain out of a molehill," Bateman said. "The fact that you and your partner grabbed a book from a crime scene is really no big thing. There is no law against trying to make a counterfeiting case. I just want the book returned. I'm certainly not looking to crucify anyone over this."

"I don't know what you're talking about."

"In other words you're going to sit there and deny having taken the book even though your partner has already told us the truth about the incident?" Bateman said.

"I don't know what else to tell you."

The conversation went on like this for another twenty minutes or so. Lindberg sat restlessly, smoked another cigarette. Finally he stood up. The meeting was over.

Richard Chance returned to the bullpen and took a seat at the desk across from Vukovich. He winked. Aware that Bateman may have bugged the office, the partners worked perfunctorily for the next couple of hours, limiting their conversation to small talk as they filled in forms and returned phone calls.

At 11:30 one of the Field Office squad leaders called some names over the office intercom. Some of the agents left their desks and headed to a briefing room across the hall from the bullpen. A short time later the same agents wandered to a steel gun cabinet in the corner of the room, signed out equipment and loaded shotguns before fitting them into leather cases. Two by two, they left the office.

As Vukovich and Chance were leaving to go to lunch, Bateman came out of his office into the hallway and asked Vukovich to step inside. Bateman closed the door. As if he needed to be shielded before he spoke, he rushed to take a seat behind his desk. "Speaking man to man," he said, "I don't really give a rat's ass if you nabbed that book. The police brass made an issue of it, probably because they're looking for a scapegoat in case they can't solve Waxman's murder. I couldn't refuse to let them interview you. One of my responsibilities as agent-in-charge is to keep the local cops happy; to maintain a proper *interface* with these people.''

"No hard feelings," Vukovich said. *You goddamn snake.*

"I think it's relevant that I've had three other agents refuse to work with Chance since he transferred in," Bateman said. "They've come right in here and refused to work with the man. I guess you're aware of that.''

Vukovich nodded.

"I hope you don't think I didn't back you up today. I don't want anyone in this Field Office to get the impression that I don't back my men.''

"You wouldn't know *how* to back anyone up," Vukovich said. He felt blood rush to his face.

"There's no need to be hostile. I have a job to do. I have certain responsibilities. I'm being very truthful when I tell you that I could totally care less if you took Waxman's book.''

"Bullshit," Vukovich said.

"I think it's best if we end this conversation right here.''

Vukovich left the room and found Chance waiting in the hall near the elevator; the partners stood silently until it arrived. Chance took his time lighting a cigarette as the elevator began its descent. "Bateman tried to trick me into copping out by saying you admitted we'd both been inside the law office," Chance said. He dropped the match on the floor. "The dumb fuck actually expected me to believe it.'' The elevator door opened.

"And what did you say?" Vukovich said as he stepped out of the elevator into the underground garage.

"I told him that if you'd said that you were a liar," Chance said. "The homicide dick looked like he wanted to crawl into a hole and pull it in after him.''

They drove to The Patio, a large, open-air restaurant located, oddly, in an industrial area near the juncture of the Pasadena and Golden State freeways. They parked the G-car in a spacious lot and walked into a walled courtyard filled with redwood tables surrounding a greenish fountain which, Vukovich noted, was working for once. They went through a short buffet line, paid for their meals and carried trays to a table in the corner.

"Look who's here," Chance said as they sat down.

Detective Lindberg sat a few tables away with a busty red-head Vukovich had seen before in the police records bureau. The detective stared at them for a moment. He wiped his mouth with a napkin, got up and ambled toward them.

"Here we go," Chance said under his breath.

"My captain ordered me to brief your agent-in-charge. My idea was to come to you off the record and just ask for the book back. I want you to know that." He put his hand over his mouth and belched. "I also want you to know that I think you snatched the book." He turned and went back to his table.

"My motto is *Never Cop Out*," Chance said when the detective was out of earshot. "I'm an N-C-O to the end."

"You shouldn't have done it," Vuckovich said between bites.

"That's second guessing."

They lingered over their meal and, though Vukovich wasn't that hungry, he followed Chance back to the buffet line. Both men filled their plates for a second time. They returned to their table and, surrounded by the sound of luncheon conversation, the gurgling cement fountain and the freeway, they ate till they were stuffed.

CHAPTER SEVEN

After putting in a full day at the Field Office Richard Chance drove to Hollywood.

He cruised down Sunset Boulevard through a commercial district consisting of sex shops, porno theaters and stores which sold magic tricks and masks, leather goods and lingerie. The sidewalks were crowded with the usual mixture of teenage hookers and runaways, men wearing tight trousers and tennis shoes and forlorn-looking tourists.

As he neared the gaudy pseudo-oriental facade of Grauman's Chinese Theater, he turned left into a neighborhood of prewar homes and newer apartment houses, which he knew were frequently burglarized by the Hollywood street people. He parked the government sedan at the curb in front of a six-story apartment house, climbed out and made his way to one of the apartments. Using his key, he unlocked the door and went in.

"Who's there?" Ruthie the Rat called from the bedroom.

"Me."

He closed the door behind him, walked over to a well-stocked mahogany bar in the corner of the room and poured himself a scotch. The sofas in the spacious living room were decorated with colorful oversized pillows, and the walls were covered with framed prints and posters: a skin-suited rock star screaming into a microphone, a pink ostrich, a blue-tinted Picasso print depicting sad people standing at the seashore. The window view was of another apartment house.

Chance sipped the drink, then carried it down a short hallway to a bedroom. Ruthie stood naked at the edge of her queen-sized bed drying herself with a fluffy purple towel. He stared at her protruding pelvic bones, her fist-sized, pointed breasts. Above the bed was a four-foot-square oil painting: a panorama of thick gray clouds held up by a King Kong hand.

"What's the word on the street about Max?" he said.

"Nobody knows," she said. "And nobody cares. Everyone hated him. He used to make his clients hand over their funny money and dope to pay his fee. Then he'd sell it himself. He'd plead everyone guilty rather than waste his precious time in a trial. The only ones he'd try to help were those who owed him money. He got what he deserved. That's what everyone on the street is saying. He got exactly what he deserved." She used the towel to dry her back.

"Did the book you found have Rick Master's name?" she said.

"Yep."

She bent over and dried her legs. "It's too bad in a way," she said as her tits jiggled. "If you'd have caught Max dirty, he'd have done anything for you to keep from going to the joint. It's for sure *I* did when you caught me. I just didn't want to go to prison. I would have done anything to stay out." She stood up. "Hell, I *have* done anything and everything to stay out." She smiled.

Chance took another drink of the scotch and set the glass down on the dresser. He unbuttoned his shirt and shrugged it off.

Ruthie watched him, still smiling. "It looks like Agent Chance is going to pump one of his informants for information," she said coyly.

Chance unfastened his belt and trousers and dropped them to the floor. She followed him onto the bed. They kissed perfunctorily while she massaged his cock. "They're in the drawer," she whispered.

He reached to the top drawer of the nightstand and pulled out a handful of elastic bandages, then proceeded to tie her arms to the bedposts at the top of the bed.

"Not the legs this time," she said.

He tossed the rest of the bandages on the floor. Since he had become erect as he fastened her arms, he mounted her immediately.

Ruthie pointed her legs in the air and made long, forceful moans. Chance came quickly and rolled off her onto his back. He took a few deep breaths.

"How much do I get for the info I gave you on Waxman?" she said.

"No arrest—no money."

"It's not my fault the man is dead. It took me almost a month to get next to him. I have expenses like everyone else in the world. My rent is due in three days."

"Uncle Sam doesn't really give a shit about your rent."

"Very funny," she said. "If you people would give me enough money to live on, I could stop dealing in twenties and fifties. I'd stop in a minute."

"No you wouldn't," Chance said as he stared at her reflection in the mirrored ceiling. He reached for the elastic bandage to untie her.

She shook her head to stop him. "I want to stay like this for a while."

Chance crawled off the bed and walked over to the dresser for his drink. He sat down cross-legged on the bed, facing her.

"One day someone I've set up for you is going to snuff

me out,'' she said. ''It's not that hard to figure out who the informant is.''

''They never know for sure.''

''They go to jail and I don't. It doesn't take a genius to figure it out. These people aren't dumb. In fact, some of the smartest people I've ever met in my life are people who are into the paper trip. I mean it.''

''You're not too slow yourself,'' he said casually.

''I made it by not getting involved in pissing contests. If I sold to someone and they ripped me off, I didn't lose my head and hire someone to go after them. Instead of starting a war I just never dealt with them again. I've always figured it was better to lose a little paper than get involved in something I couldn't handle. That's what happened to my husband. He got in a war with some bikers and ended up killing one of them. That's why he's doing life in Folsom. He always took things personal.''

Chance finished his drink and set the glass on the nightstand. ''Why do you like to be tied up?''

''Huh?''

''Why do you like to be tied up?''

''Lots of women like to be tied up when they get laid.''

''How do you know?''

''I read it in a book,'' she said. ''It's a fantasy thing.''

He shrugged and headed into the bathroom. He shaved and showered, used a clean towel to dry off. When he stepped back into the bedroom he noticed that her eyes were closed.

''Are you going to stay the night?'' she asked without opening them.

''No,'' he said as he pulled on his trousers. ''I have some things to do.''

''I have some info for you.''

''I'm listening.''

''The word is a big dealer from New York is coming into town in the next couple of weeks with fifty grand to buy some stolen diamonds. He's a Chinaman and he's connected to some big people in the Far East. The deal will go down at the L.A. Airport. A switch-the-locker-key act.''

"Very interesting," he said. "But it's like I've told you, I'm only interested in funny money. And I could care less about people who want to *buy*. I'm looking for people who *sell*."

She opened her eyes. "Now that Max is dead, what do you want me to do next?"

"See if you can find out who's going to take up the slack. There'll probably be a fight over his customers."

"How am I supposed to do that?"

"Ask around. Tell people that Max was your connection. Someone will tell you where to go."

"And if there *is* no back-up man?" she said. "I mean it's possible that *nobody* will try to take over his territory."

"If that's the case, then you can have it."

"Sounds challenging," she said.

"Did I ever tell you that you're a bum lay?" he said as he buttoned his shirt.

"Did I ever tell you that no man I've ever balled has turned me on as much as an electric vibrator I bought for six dollars?" She struggled with her bonds. "Untie me."

Once freed she grabbed a flimsy robe off a chair and put it on. "Sometimes I think I'd like to get the hell out of L.A." She stepped to the mirror and fluffed her hair. "I hate the smog and the freeways . . . and I hate everyone who lives here. I'd love to live at the beach . . . maybe Carmel. I've always loved Carmel. But I wouldn't want to live there if I couldn't live in one of those big ocean-view houses."

Chance stood next to her at the mirror, combing his hair.

"The same thing that happened to Max Waxman could happen to me," she said, then waited for a response.

He patted a few stray hairs into place.

"Did you hear what I said?"

"Nothing is going to happen to you."

She grabbed a brush off the dresser and ran it through her hair. "You probably couldn't care less anyway."

He grabbed the hand holding the brush and pulled her to him. He kissed her fully on the mouth. "Let's don't make more of it than it is," he whispered.

"You could get into trouble over me."

"Who's going to tell them?"

"I'm an informer."

He nuzzled her ear. "But if you inform on me, I'll put a bullet in your brain," he whispered.

She pushed him away. "I don't like it when you say things like that." More brush strokes.

Chance wandered out of the bedroom and into the kitchen. He opened the refrigerator, reached behind a plastic tray containing glass vials of cocaine and grabbed a quart bottle of orange juice. He took a long drink directly from the container and wiped his mouth with the back of his hand, then replaced the container and shut the refrigerator door.

Ruthie came into the living room. She was still brushing her hair. "May I ask you something?"

"Sure," he said as he walked to the door.

"What would you do if I stopped giving you information?"

"Why do you ask?"

She stopped brushing. "I'd just like to know."

"I'd probably have your parole violated. You'd end up in federal prison."

"Do you really mean that?"

Chance smiled as he shrugged. He gave her a little slap on the ass and walked out the door.

The L.A. Airport was a beehive of horn-honking, suitcase-dragging confusion. Whether coming or going, it seemed that everyone—cab drivers, passengers and sky caps—was in a hurry.

Richard Chance pulled up to the curb in front of a baggage area swarming with middle-aged men and women wearing flower-print shirts and wilted flower leis.

She was waiting for him, standing in a group of identically attired female flight attendants with matching valises. He turned off the engine and got out of the car. He opened the trunk and the svelte brunette stepped off the curb. She dropped her valise inside.

"I was beginning to wonder if you were stuck somewhere on a stakeout or something," she said as he slammed the lid down.

"I was. I've got to get back as soon as I can." *What the hell is her name?* he thought when he realized it had slipped his mind. He opened the passenger door for her. As she climbed in he noticed that her name tag read S. Williams. *Susan? Sharon? Sherri?*

She gave him a playful poke on the shoulder. "I didn't think you were going to call," she said. "Men always take numbers and never call. And policemen are the worst." She paused for a moment. "You look preoccupied."

"Lots of things on my mind." *Sally? Sandy?*

"One of the other flight attendants said you fellas always seem to find out when Mary has one of her parties," she said. "By the way, how well do you know her?"

"We went to dinner once," he said, matter-of-factly. *And I ate her box for dessert.* He realized that he'd left his address book at the Field Office . . . it would do no good to use the excuse of making a phone call so he could look up her name.

She gave directions to her apartment in Hermosa Beach, and when they pulled up in front of a wood-frame duplex he carried her luggage inside. The apartment was walking distance to the beach.

"Do you have time for a drink before you rush back to work?" she asked as she opened windows and pulled drapes.

"Sure," he said. The living room was small and tastefully decorated; a wall unit with an arrangement of artificial flowers and stereo gear; some thick shag throw rugs and Hawaiian wood carvings.

"What did Mary tell you about me?"

"Nothing much," he said. "You were on the same flight crew or something like that." *And that you'd just broken up with your pilot boyfriend and were horny as hell.*

They sat down on a sofa after she'd made drinks. She made more small talk: which T-men she liked, which T-men she didn't like, how similar were the lives of Feds and flight attendants. As she spoke, he made little interviewer nods and tried to think of her name. When he noticed a postcard on the coffee table which was addressed to Samantha Williams he felt like cheering.

"I like you, Samantha."

"I like you, too."

"Funny," he said, "how we just sort of hit it off at that party." He took her hand, kissed it, and pulled her to him. He tried to kiss her but she avoided his lips and nestled her head on his shoulder.

"I don't think I'm ready for a relationship at this point," she said softly.

"I am."

"You don't even know me."

Gently, he pulled her head back and kissed her. He ran his hand between her thighs.

"Please don't," she murmured.

He felt the warmth between her legs and she reached for him. He carried her into the bedroom and they undressed each other. She had thin, cameo shoulders and firm breasts, legs and stomach.

They embraced and crawled onto the bed.

After a half hour or so of sex, she reached up and used both hands to wipe his brow. "I want you to come," she said, kissing his forehead.

He continued to thrust gently. It was the way he treated all women the first time: make them come back for seconds. He breathed harder, then finally, with a rapid crescendo of short, violent strokes, he seared into orgasm.

Samantha yelped a few times, which he figured she did to please him. Because he knew that most women liked it, he held her tightly, nuzzling her for a while.

"Is your job dangerous?" she said.

"I don't think about it," he said as he wondered whether she had herpes or gonorrhea.

She kissed him on the cheek.

After what he felt was an appropriate amount of time, he climbed out of the bed and showered. As he soaped up, he realized it was his third shower of the day. Busy life, he thought to himself.

By the time he finished, Samantha had dressed. She wore a halter top and a pair of tennis shorts that were a size too small.

"Gotta run," he said, as he pulled on his shirt and trousers.

"I wish you could stay for a while," she said.

"Gotta get back to work. Big stakeout. . . . Maybe we can get together on the weekend."

"I'd like that."

She followed him to the front door. He opened it and turned to her. Taking her face in his hands, he kissed her on the lips. "I like you," he said.

"Please call me."

"I promise," he said, then trotted to his car.

The trip to the Seafarer Restaurant, an overpriced lobster house in Beverly Hills, took him less than twenty minutes. He pulled under a canopy in front and tossed his car keys to a valet-parking attendant wearing a blue jumpsuit. He hurried through a front door decorated with a coiled-rope anchor. Joan Russel, an attractive, forty-five-year-old red-haired woman whose only physical drawbacks were excessive makeup and a broad secretarial ass, sat alone at the bar. She wore a beige business suit and a yellow scarf.

"I tried to call," he said apologetically as he sat down on the bar stool next to her. "I'm sorry I'm late. I really am."

"I can't believe I'm still sitting here," she said to her martini. She spoke in a drunken slur.

"I've been running a hundred miles an hour all day," he said.

The bartender brought the drinks; Chance fumbled for his wallet. She told the bartender to put the drinks on her tab.

Chance leaned close to her, kissed her on the nape of the neck. She rested her head on his shoulder, then sat up and took a big sip of her martini. "I think the only reason you call me is because I have a big expense account," she said.

He gritted his teeth as if he were offended. *Let's eat, bitch.*

"I didn't mean that," she said quickly, seeing his look, and kissed him on the cheek.

By the time they'd been seated in the restaurant and served their salads she was in slightly better spirits. He ordered expensive wine for the entree.

"I wish you would give me more than a few hours notice," she said. "You always call me at the last minute."

"I never know from one day to the next."

"I think you like the idea of not knowing from one day to the next. Cops are all crazy."

He shrugged. They made small talk as they ate, followed by a long silence as they waited for the main course.

"We have nothing in common," she said finally. "It's not just that you're younger than I am. It's that we really have nothing in common."

He tried to change the subject as the waiter served the lobster and refilled wine glasses for the third time, but she continued. "Generally, you treat me like a whore," she said after the waiter left. "Isn't that what they say? Treat a lady like a whore and a whore like a lady?"

Ignoring her, he dipped lobster into drawn butter and took a bite.

"I'm sorry I'm acting like this," she said.

"You have every right to be angry," he said as he cracked a claw.

By the time they finished eating, her mood had lifted considerably. The waiter served an expensive dessert wine, and he ruminated over whether he would punish her by kissing her goodnight in the parking lot or follow her home and make the day three for three.

"What are you thinking about?" she said, seeming to become moody again.

"About getting into your pants."

Her look of dismay turned to a smile. She laughed. He made a show of trying to pay when the waiter brought the bill, but gave in when she tossed her company credit card on the table.

Later in bed as she blew him, he told her that his difficulty in getting an erection was due to exhaustion from work. She grunted in response as her head continued to plunge between his legs. He closed his eyes and concentrated. Finally, he was erect. By the time he climaxed, they were both soaked with perspiration.

As she dropped off to sleep, he climbed off the bed and did three sets of push-ups, fifty each. He took his fourth shower for the day and left.

Driving back to his apartment, he mused sleepily over the events of the day. All in all, he'd accomplished everything he'd wanted to do. To avoid falling asleep at the wheel, he turned on the radio to a rock station and adjusted the volume to an ear-shattering level.

CHAPTER EIGHT

The next day, Jim Hart plugged in the Field Office coffee pot and headed into the bullpen. As he passed by Vukovich's desk, he wondered how he'd weathered the beef the day before. Though he knew it was really none of his business, he promised himself that he would ask as soon as Vukovich came in.

Seated at his desk, Hart opened a newspaper and read for a while. Secretaries and agents said good morning as they passed by the door or came into the office. The coffee perked.

The phone rang; Hart picked up the receiver.

"Bob Grimes here," the voice said, recognizing Hart. "Are you *very* busy today?"

"I do my best never to be busy," Hart said.

"Do you suppose we could get together for a few minutes? I need to talk something over with you."

"I guess," Hart said hesitantly. "I'll be in the office until. . . ."

"I'd rather not come to your office if you don't mind," Grimes said.

"What's up?"

"I can't really talk over the phone. Can you meet me at the Jade Pagoda at one? It'll just take a few minutes."

"See you there," Hart said. He set the receiver down. Having finished the newspaper, he walked over to a computer in the corner of the room. Referring to directions which were posted above the machine, he entered the name Robert Grimes. A case number appeared on the computer screen. He wrote the number down.

At a file cabinet on the opposite side of the room, he located a thick intelligence file bearing the case number. He returned to his desk with the file and began leafing through. The file concerned a surveillance on Rick Masters who was described in the file as an OCF (Organized Crime Figure). Surveillance logs showed that Masters, as well as keeping appointments with various members of the L.A. underworld, met almost daily with Grimes, his lawyer. Hart found a large manila envelope in the file. He opened it and pulled out a stack of 8″ × 11″ color surveillance photographs. One showed the lanky Masters entering an office building accompanied by a Latin woman with alluring features: piercing, dark eyes, full lips, wide mouth and a swept-up bouffant hair-do which accentuated her high cheekbones. She was dressed in a slim skirt and loose-fitting blouse which hung open enough to reveal a startling cleavage. Someone had scrawled *Entering Office w/ Girlfriend* across the white border on the top of the photo. Hart closed the file and returned it to the cabinet.

After a trip to the office tech room, Jim Hart left the office and spent the rest of the morning completing errands. He picked up his laundry, got his hair cut and browsed at Reels, a downtown fishing tackle shop.

At one o'clock Jim Hart sat at a window seat in the dimly lit upstairs bar of the Jade Pagoda Restaurant, a musty Chinatown palace whose red-and-black paneled walls were dec-

orated with Chinese cork art. A boisterous lunch crowd of
civil service workers from downtown government buildings
and a few tourists was starting to thin out.

Hart sipped from a cocktail glass filled with straight ginger ale (he'd stopped drinking after his wife died because he
feared a slide into alcoholism) and stared out the window.

Below him, tourists of all ages wandered in and out of
Chinatown's myriad of tiny gift shops which were built
along a red-brick plaza and the neon-lined walking streets
leading from it: identical establishments which Hart knew
smelled of incense and sold plastic Buddhas, paper parasols,
colorful scarves and tourist postcards which invariably de-
picted a Chinatown of bright colors under clear blue skies
rather than as it really was, generally run-down and blanketed with smog.

Hart glanced at his wristwatch. Grimes was late, which
he didn't consider the least bit unusual. It had been his expe-
rience that lawyers were always late, particularly to court.
He chalked it up to ego.

The bartender, a flat-faced Oriental man with pouting lips
and large abdomen, left the bar carrying a tray of drinks. He
served an overweight couple sitting at a table in the corner
and returned to the bar.

A black limousine pulled up to the entrance of the plaza
and parked directly in front of a fire hydrant. A young
chauffeur with shoulder-length hair jumped out of the limousine and scurried to the passenger side. He opened the
door. Robert Grimes, a well-fed and tanned man of Hart's
age, climbed out of the limousine and said something to the
chauffeur. After touching his salt-and-pepper hair in a couple of places to see if it was still in place, he adjusted his
cufflinks. He strode across the plaza toward the Jade Pagoda
Restaurant.

Grimes emerged from the stairwell a moment later, looking around the room. Hart waved. Grimes came to the table
and they shook hands.

"I'm glad we could get together," he said as he sat down. "Sometimes it seems like life is just rushing by at a hundred miles an hour . . . no time for old friends." He looked at Hart as if they actually had been more than just co-workers for a few years. "It seems like just yesterday I was an agent working in the Field Office and going to law school at night."

"If you'd have stayed you and I would have been able to retire at the same time," Hart said. "That would have been nice."

Grimes smiled as he leaned forward. "You're still a sweet-talker," he said. "You sweet-talk those counterfeiters right into Terminal Island." He smiled amiably. "Hell, I guess patience is ninety percent of it. You'd play with the crooks' minds to get 'em to cop out. I was too impatient. I'd want to slap 'em around the interrogation room to make 'em talk. Impatient. I guess that's the best way to describe it. I was impatient. The thought of having to fill out a form just to get a box of paper clips still gives me a headache. Bureaucracy, that's what finally made me quit. The pure bullshit bureaucracy, the eraserheads that always end up being promoted to agent-in-charge. I couldn't hack taking orders. Besides, law enforcement is a pit. The harder you work, the more cases an agent brings to the U.S. Attorney's office, the more chances there are to get in trouble. I like it on this side of the street. The more effort I put in, the more money I make."

Hart noticed the diamond stud cufflinks as Grimes pushed a sleeve back and checked a Rolex. "I don't have long," he said. "I'm in the middle of a trial." He turned towards the bar. "Scotch water, please," he said in his best command voice. The bartender nodded.

"What kind of trial?" Hart asked.

"A dope case. My client got caught delivering a pound of nose candy. I should be able to get him off, though. The search warrant is weak."

"Weak?"

"The color of the house is listed as brown in the warrant when it is in fact beige and yellow," Grimes said.

Hart shook his head. "You should be ashamed of yourself."

The bartender came to the table, set down the drink. "I make no apologies for being an attorney at law," Grimes said. "Everyone deserves a good defense. Besides, if I wouldn't have accepted the case, someone else would have . . . *without a doubt.*" He drank the scotch and set the glass down.

Hart smiled. "Without a doubt."

"That's not to say that I'm in love with dope pushers and funny money dealers. Doctors make money off cancer. That doesn't mean they *like* it."

"Can't argue that one," Hart agreed, avoiding confrontation.

Grimes pointed out the window. On the street below, his chauffeur wiped the windshield of the limousine with a cloth.

"Masters has taken to phoning me in the middle of the night and ordering me around like I was one of his mules. The other day he even had the balls to *threaten* me."

"About what?"

"The man is an animal," Grimes said, ignoring the question. "I own a home in Beverly Hills right now because of defending people like him, but that doesn't make me *like* them."

Hart drank the ginger ale and wished it was bourbon.

"I know you fellas at the Field Office refer to me as a mob attorney. Even the L.A. *Times* has called me that a time or two. But, believe it or not, I'm still on the side of law and order. I'm basically a square; an establishment square. Sure, I'll admit to a few compromises here and there, but compromises are the price of success. Don't you agree?"

"Usually," Hart said.

"I'm as good a defense attorney as I was a Treasury agent, and later a federal prosecutor," Grimes said. "There is nothing immoral in this. It's the adversary system. People have a right to a good defense." As if he realized he was repeating himself, he stopped for a moment, finished his drink and rattled the ice in the glass. "Here I am apologizing for having made myself rich." He laughed.

Hart forced himself to join the laughter as he waited for Grimes to get to the point.

"But that isn't to say I haven't paid a price. Frankly, being house counsel for a counterfeiter doesn't sit well with me. As a matter of fact, I'm up to here with it." He held his hand under his chin. "I'm up to here with crooks."

"So am I. That's why I'm going to retire in a couple of months."

Grimes motioned to the bartender for another drink. He settled back in his chair. "How would you like to make the biggest case of your career before you retire?"

Hart waited a beat before answering.

"I'm listening."

Grimes glanced around the room, leaned forward with his elbows on the table. "How would you like to lock up Rick Masters?" he whispered.

"How?"

"He tells me things that would be of great use to you."

"I'm still listening."

"All I would ask is that you give me your personal word of honor that you will never reveal my name as an informant. I needn't explain what would happen to my career as a defense lawyer if there was even a hint that I'd set up one of my own clients." He stopped talking as a man and woman walked past them toward the stairs.

"Why do you want to set up your best client?" Hart said.

"Let's just say I'm tired of being his legal lackey and since he's the type of person who thinks he owns everyone around him, there's no other way for me to sever the relationship . . . I bet I can guess your next question.''

Hart regarded him with an amused expression.

''You were going to ask me, since I know most of the agents in the L.A. office, why I came to *you*.''

''You guessed it,'' Hart said.

Grimes stirred ice with a cocktail straw. ''I came to you because years ago you never let anyone know the identity of your informants. Even when I became assistant U.S. attorney and had a right to know, you *still* refused to tell me. Do you remember how angry I used to get?''

''Never forgot it,'' Hart said, though he had.

Grimes glanced at his wristwatch again. ''And since Masters has beaten you in court three for three during the last ten years, I figure you owe him one.''

''You have my word your name won't come out.''

''I have your solid, honest-to-Christ word?''

''You have my word.''

The bartender brought Grimes another drink; he paid for it and took a long, slow sip, then set the glass down carefully. ''The first thing you should do is talk to a hood named Carmine Falcone,'' he said. ''He's serving time in Terminal Island. He got caught at the airport with forty grand worth of Masters's hundreds. The U.S. attorney offered him immunity to testify against Masters. Falcone refused the offer because Masters promised to pull strings with a federal judge and get him released. Well, Masters couldn't come through and Falcone is screaming bloody murder.''

''How do you know all this?''

''I defended him. Masters paid my retainer. Masters is very worried about him. *Very* worried.''

''Do you think Falcone is angry enough at Masters to set him up for me?'' Hart asked.

''That depends on how much sweet talk you can put forth. The man wants out of the joint.''

Hart nodded.

"I want you to know that when you retire I have an investigator's position waiting for you. Working for my firm you'll make twice what you do now, plus an expense account, car, the works. This, of course, has nothing to do with what we've talked about today, but I wanted you to know that the job is waiting for you."

"I appreciate the offer, Bob, but when I retire, I'll be heading up north to go fishing. Hell, I may never come back."

"Bagging Masters would be a fruitful end to your career," he said. "A real swan song. I wish you luck." They shook hands across the table. Grimes made a comment about being late for court, stood up and slapped Hart on the back. "You and your damn fishing," he said and headed down the stairs.

Hart watched out the windows as Grimes ambled across the plaza past a wishing well ornamented with cheap Oriental figurines. He waited until the limousine drove off, paid his bar tab and made his way down the steps and out the door.

Taking his time, Hart strolled past pagodaed curio shops and restaurants to Hill Street. He waited for the light to turn green, then crossed the street and got into his car. He glanced around carefully, then removed his suit coat and tossed it onto the back seat. He unbuttoned his shirt and carefully pulled off the patches of surgical tape which held a tiny skin-colored microphone in place in the middle of his chest. After unplugging similarly colored wire leading from the microphone to a cigarette-case-sized tape recorder that was secured to his waist, he removed the lid to the recorder, ejected the miniature tape cassette and dropped it in his shirt pocket.

Jim Hart started the car and drove to a downtown bank where he often cashed his government paychecks. There, he placed the tape cassette in a safe deposit box containing family records which, other than himself, only his daughter and son-in-law knew about.

His errand completed, he returned to the Field Office and reviewed the file on Carmine Falcone. It was filled with copies of offer-of-immunity correspondence from the U.S. attorney, an investigative report which outlined Falcone's arrest at the airport (an anonymous male caller had phoned in the tip that Falcone was heading to Las Vegas with counterfeit money) and routine arrest paperwork: mug shots, evidence forms, contraband inventories. By the time he'd completed reviewing the file it was almost six o'clock.

On his way home that night he stopped at a supermarket and bought canned Spam, cheese, bread and beer. After making sandwiches he sat alone, eating in front of the television set, paying little attention to the programs that played themselves out.

As he crawled into bed that night, he was still trying to figure out what Grimes was up to.

CHAPTER NINE

Rick Masters sat with Blanca at one of the tables which lined the bay window in Pepe's. The view encompassed the spectacle of sailboats and other pleasure craft parading about on the Marina Del Rey, a man-made harbor which, if one believed the environmentalists, was polluted because of sewage floating south from Santa Monica. The bar was a franchised operation with an early California motif. Its walls were plastered in places with a synthetic adobe brick for the "weathered" look. Stiff white sombreros and matching leather gun belts hung on horizontal coatracks which were too high to reach. The customers, like guests at a costume ball, were dressed in perfectly-pressed tennis, jogging and yachting outfits.

Rick Masters sipped his marguerita, set the glass down and twirled it gently in a ring of moisture.

Blanca fidgeted. "How long are we gonna wait?"

"Till he gets here."

"I hate waiting," she said.

"It's the way these people are. They run on their own time." As he spoke, raising his voice to be heard, he became aware of the animated conversation in the now-crowded bar. It was the standard beach bullshit: the price of property, jazz, who was balling who, health food, the price of boats.

A tall black man sauntered into the bar. He wore a gray business suit and red silk tie and eyeglasses with thick black frames. His hair was closely cropped and he had a well-trimmed mustache and goatee. Though he nodded to acknowledge Masters's presence, he nevertheless surveyed the bar carefully before approaching the table.

Masters did the soul handshake with him and offered a seat at the table. The man stared at Blanca for a moment.

"I don't talk business in front of no woman," he said.

Blanca glared.

Masters winked at her. Maintaining her glare at the black man, she stood up and headed to the bar.

"I hope your bitch don't get mad, but you see I don't trust anything that can bleed for seven days and don't die," the black man said as he sat down.

"A drink?" Masters said.

" 'Gainst my religion."

"How did the last stuff go?"

"I done had it sold within a week. I need more, but you done changed all your phone numbers . . . I musta called you a hundred mothafuckin times. I had people begging me for some of them fifties. Mothafuckin *begging* me."

"I had a problem. I had to lay low for a while."

"That's what I heard. I heard your mule, the Eye-talian boy, got popped at the airport."

"He took the case to trial and lost. The judge gave him five years."

Suddenly a group of tanned, tennis-togged women sitting at the next table broke into laughter over something. One of the women spilled a drink. A wispy blonde waitress dressed in a red flamenco costume came to the table. She used napkins to wipe up the spill. After completing the cleanup she turned and asked Masters if he wanted another round. He shook his head. The black man ordered a coke. The waitress frowned and rushed off.

"That's what I wanted to talk about," Masters said.

"Whatsat?"

"Carmine Falcone. I'm worried about him."

The black man leaned forward. "How you be worried about him?"

Masters moved back slightly because he could smell his breath. "He's in Terminal Island and I'm worried that he might try to deal his way out."

"You worried that the man might snitch to the Feds."

Masters nodded. "He could hurt both of us."

"The mothafucka can say what he want about me. I never went hand to hand. I always had him deliver it to a phone booth. I had my own mule pick it up. He can say whatever the fuck he wants to say about me."

"On the other hand, he knew you were the one who was paying for the paper. He used to collect buy money from you. I'm sure you'll agree that this is something the Feds would love to know."

The waitress returned to the table, set a coke in a tall glass in front of the black man. Masters paid and gave her a five dollar tip. She smiled and hurried off.

"I think I see where you be coming from," the black man said, sipping the drink. "You *worried* about the man."

"How much of a problem would it be?" Masters said.

"One of the brothers could take care of it. It ain't no big thing . . . but ain't no brother going to work for free."

"How much would it take?"

The black man sat back in his chair. "Depends on what you going to pay with."

"What the hell do you *think* I'm going to pay with?"

"It'll cost you a hundred thousand . . . a hundred K in

twenties—that is if they be as good as the last ones you made up.''

''Fifty grand in hundreds. That's all I have on hand right at the moment. That's the best I can do.''

The black man slowly shook his head back and forth. ''Them big bills ain't very popular with the brother,'' he said. ''Hamburger stands and little markets where the brother down his paper won't accept no big bills from a black man. The onlies people that like them fifties and hundreds is dope fiends. They throw a few in their buy money now and then to make it go farther. It's got to be twenties. I cain't use nothin bigger.''

''Now that I think of it I might have about fifty grand or so in twenties lying around somewhere.'' Masters said after pausing for a moment.

The black man shook his head in dismay. ''Can I axe you something?''

Masters lifted his eyebrows.

''Since you print that shit your *own* self, what the fuck would you care if I got fifty grand or a hundred grand? To you it be nothing but mothafuckin *paper*. I'll take seventy-five K in twenties and I personally guarantee the job.''

''If anything goes wrong and Falcone lives, we'll both be in trouble,'' Masters said. ''He'll know what was going down. He'll sing like a bird.''

''Don't be worrying yourself none. He ain't gonna live. The man *ain't gonna* live.''

''And you are accepting the responsibility?''

''Isn't that what I just mothafuckin *said*?''

Masters finished his drink.

''I'll need some money up front,'' the black man said.

''I don't deal up front. You've been around me long enough to know that.''

''This is different. I have to show certain people that this thing is for real. It's not easy to get to a man when he's in the joint. If it was, you wouldn't be sitting here talking with me right now."

"You've accepted the responsibility. Put up your own front money. I'll pay you within eight hours of the time I confirm he's dead. I personally guarantee that the package is waiting."

The black man bit his lip, reached into his coat and took out a pen. He slid the cocktail napkin from under his drink.

"Carmine Falcone, F-A-L-C-O-N-E," Masters said. "He's in module twelve. His prison number is . . ." He removed a card from his shirt pocket and read the number slowly, then repeated it as the black man made notes.

The black man read the number back, put the pen away and folded the napkin. He stuffed it into a coat pocket.

"What kind of a time factor am I looking at?" Masters asked.

"It'll take a week or two. These things have to be done right. But don't you worry none. The mothafucker is as good as dead." With that, he stood up and walked out of the bar.

Blanca returned to the table. She sat with her arms folded across her chest, her mouth in a straight line.

"You shouldn't let people like that bother you," he said.

Tears welled in her eyes. "Why did you let him talk to me like that?" she said angrily.

"Because I need him. There's no other way to get Carmine."

"I'm not a whore," she hissed. "You can say what you want about me. I've done dope and I've stripped on a stage, but I've never sold my ass. I don't deserve to be treated like somebody's goddamn *puta*. Particularly by some *penche cabron miate*. I should have spit right in his face."

He stood up and took her hand. "Just forget about it," he said as they walked toward the door.

"I'd like to make him kiss my ass," she said. "Actually get down on his knees and kiss my ass."

Nothing was said as Masters drove the Rolls east on the Marina freeway. A few miles later he swung into a transition road which fed into a freeway leading to West Los Angeles.

"Tomorrow I want you to go down to Terminal Island and see Carmine," Masters said. "Tell him that I was finally able to get to the judge. Tell him that his case has been fixed and I'll have him out within a couple of weeks. Tell him I'm going to make the payoff to the judge's old law partner and that the fix is definitely in."

She nodded. "What is the best restaurant in Beverly Hills?"

"Probably Ma Maison," he said.

"That's where I want to go tonight."

"What's in it for me?" Masters said.

"When we get home I'll let you come all over my face."

"Sounds like a deal," he said.

It was Friday.

Vukovich had spent the entire day at the U.S. courthouse sitting in a waiting room outside the chambers of the Los Angeles Grand Jury to testify in a two-year-old counterfeiting case. Shortly after 5 P.M., an assistant U.S. attorney, who, with cigar and tails could have doubled for a youthful Groucho Marx, stepped out of the meeting room carrying a sheaf of legal papers.

"I decided your testimony wasn't necessary after all," he said as he passed by on his way to the elevator. The prosecutor pushed the elevator button, the door opened. "Sorry about that," he said as he adjusted the paperwork from one arm to another and stepped inside.

Vukovich walked toward the elevator. As he was about to step on, the doors closed in his face. Though he felt like pulling his gun and shooting the doors open, he simply waited for the next elevator. He needed a drink.

After returning to the Field Office and signing out for the day, he drove to the Angel's Flight. Inside the juke box was playing a country-and-western tune. The crowd was a mixture of elderly alcoholics from the decaying local neighborhood, policemen, detectives and a few agents from the office. An obese, pock-marked redhead, one of a platoon of police groupies that frequented the place, sat in her usual seat at the corner of the bar. If he remembered right her rumored specialty was four men at a time—never more and never less.

Chance waved at him from a booth in the corner. Vukovich bought a beer at the bar before he joined him.

"Was I right?" Chance said.

"Yep. I was never called to testify."

"Figures."

"What's new?" Vukovich said.

"I balled three broads last night," Chance said, smiling. "I almost didn't make the last lap."

Vukovich chuckled. "Anyone I know?"

"An airhead stewardess I met at a party last week, a sloppy executive bitch and Ruthie the Rat. All I got out of the whole evening was a free dinner and a sore dick."

"You're kidding about Ruthie, I hope."

Chance shook his head. "She's not a bad piece," he said. "A little kinky, but all and all an acceptable piece of ass; seven or eight on a ten scale."

"She could get you fired."

"She has more to lose than I do," Chance said. "She's put sixteen dealers in the joint. Any one of them would have her wasted if they found out she was an informant."

Vukovich drank his beer, mildly annoyed.

"As a matter of fact, I just spoke with her a few minutes ago," Chance said. "She says the word on the street is that Rick Masters might be good for the hit on Wax-man.''

"The untouchable Rick Masters."

"I checked his intelligence file. He's in with a lot of Hollywood types: coke-heads and wanna-be stuntmen and actors. It's a typical file. Lots of bullshit report, but no action."

Vukovich noticed a crude poster balanced on top of the cash register featuring a drawing of a stick-man jumping off a bridge. Across the bottom of the poster was scrawled *"Dick Chance Does It."* Vukovich pointed at the poster. "Dick Chance does what?"

"Tonight's the night I jump off the Vincent-Thomas Bridge. Ed O'Brien from Federal Narcotics bet me his paycheck that I won't do it."

"You're really gonna do it?" Vukovich said more as a simple statement than a question.

"It's all worked out. Ruthie will pick me up in her speedboat . . . hell, you're an ex-paratrooper. Why don't you jump with me?"

"I haven't jumped since I was in the army."

"Jumping doesn't change."

"I don't have a chute," Vukovich said, hoping it would end the discussion.

"I have an extra chute and gear in my car right now."

"How high is the bridge?"

"It's high enough for chute time. I've checked everything out."

"What type of parachutes do you have?"

"Clouds. They open flat and have great forward speed."

"Who packed 'em?"

"Packed 'em both myself."

"Lots of things can go wrong."

Chance smiled. "That's all part of it."

"You're actually nuts, do you know that?"

"If you'll jump with me, I'll split O'Brien's paycheck with you," Chance said.

As Vukovich considered the crazy offer, Chance motioned to the bartender. He ordered double shots.

"If I were you I'd be drinking straight out of the bottle right now," he said.

Chance smiled broadly.

CHAPTER TEN

It was almost midnight and it was chilly. The crowd of thirty or so federal and local cops and their girlfriends cheered raucously when they arrived at the Ports of Call village parking lot in San Pedro. Everyone was standing around cars holding beer cans. To the north of them the Vincent-Thomas Bridge loomed in the distance. Like a circus ringmaster, Chance announced that Vukovich would be making the jump with him and the drunken crowd let out another cheer. Chance and Ed O'Brien (who looked slightly dejected, probably because Chance had shown up) had a short discussion during which Chance agreed that the stocky, red-haired Irishman could have Chance's car if he was killed in the jump. A police car driven by a cop someone knew pulled up and after another short discussion the cop left to block off the bridge. Chance and Vukovich went down to check with Ruthie, who was waiting at the boat dock. Chance gave her final instructions before she climbed into the speedboat and raced off into the darkness. They returned to the car and put on parachutes, then tied waterproof flashlights that Chance had brought along to their waists.

Barefoot and in harness, they climbed into the back of a pickup truck driven by a vice cop wearing a cowboy hat. He drove them to the middle of the bridge; a parade of cars followed. In the middle of the bridge the truck stopped and everyone climbed out of cars. As Vukovich's feet touched the asphalt a chill pierced through him. By sheer will power he stopped himself from shaking and followed Chance to the bridge rail. A frigid wind whipped around them, seeming to dry his eyes. The crowd became quiet as the two agents stood at the rail. Vukovich imagined himself unsnapping his parachute harness and telling everyone he'd changed his mind. He looked down into sheer blackness outlined by harbor lights.

Without a word, Chance climbed up on the rail. One of the women turned away in fright.

"This is crazy," O'Brien said with a look of fear on his face.

"Make sure you get to full velocity before you pull," Chance said to Vukovich without taking his eyes off the harbor. He vaulted forward into the blackness and disappeared. The crowd gasped. A wave of nauseous fear overtook Vukovich as he climbed onto the guard rail. As he jumped he realized he'd forgotten to cross himself. Resisting the survival urge to pull the rip cord immediately, he fell into the soundless abyss. He tugged the rip cord and felt the pack flutter behind him and screamed until he felt the powerful tug that meant the canopy had opened. He descended quickly, the wind whipping him to and fro. As he hit the water he yanked the quick-release hook on the parachute, freeing him of the harness. Freezing water smacked him in the face. The canopy spread over him in the choppy, heaving water; Vukovich fought to get from under it, but couldn't. In a panic he punched at the chute covering him. Nothing worked. It was everywhere, drowning him, he was gagging on sea water. Holding his breath he dove underwater and swam, lifted his head. He was still under the canopy. Lungs bursting, he tried again. He coughed and sea water filled his mouth and nose. He was drowning.

Suddenly Vukovich felt something grasp his arm and pull. He was out from under the canopy, gulping air.

"Rope!" he heard Chance scream.

Vukovich fumbled for the rope, coughing as he tried to catch his breath. With Chance's help, he made it into the rocking speedboat. Vukovich flopped back in relief.

"We did it, partner! We did it!" Chance said over and over again as Ruthie sped them back to the dock. The party afterward at the Angel's Flight bar lasted until the sun came up.

Because Rick Masters had left L.A. at 4 A.M., the road to Las Vegas had been relatively traffic free. Dressed in a pair of blue mechanic's overalls, he handled the Porsche as if he were driving a race car, with his thumb lightly resting on the steering wheel . . . better for control. Seeing that the road behind was clear, he slammed the accelerator to the floor. As the machine reached eighty, ninety, then a hundred miles an hour, he concentrated on the ribbon of highway ahead. One hundred twenty, one hundred thirty. Steady.

He didn't slow down until he saw the neon outline of the city in the distance. He checked his wristwatch. L.A. to Las Vegas in three hours. He'd made the trip in record time. As he cruised slowly down the Las Vegas strip he watched bleary-eyed gamblers shuffling in and out of well-lit casinos. Gambling degenerates, he thought to himself.

Before reaching the downtown area he pulled into an enormous parking lot adjoining the Dunes hotel, climbed out of the car and removed a small black suitcase from the trunk. After locking the car he walked to a taxi stand at the front of the hotel. He quickly got into the back seat of the first cab in line, startling the driver awake.

"Thirteen eight four Paradise Valley," Masters said.

The driver turned his head, looked puzzled. "Is that the junkyard?"

Masters shook his head. "The industrial park right next to it."

"You got it," the driver said as he started the engine. The trip through the twenty-four-hour-a-day town took about ten minutes. The driver pulled up in front of a rectangular, one-story cement block building divided into separate, garage-doored enclosures. The building was surrounded by a chain-link fence. A metal sign attached to the fence read: "Industrial Storage Space for Rent." Masters paid the driver and got out of the taxi, then used a card-key to open one of the gates. Inside he used another key to open a pad-lock affixed to the door of a unit at the far end of the building. He hoisted the door, stepped inside. The cement floor of the cubicle was bare. In fact the room was empty except for several electrical outlets and a telephone which he had ordered earlier. Masters set the suitcase on the floor, un-locked it and removed a metal sign which read: Truman Printing Co.—Distinctive Stationery. He hung the sign on the wall, shut the suitcase and shoved it into a corner of the room.

A horn sounded; Masters stepped outside. A moving van was parked in front. Its passenger door opened and a husky, middle-aged man with enormous arms climbed out. "Mr. Truman?" he shouted as he approached the fence.

"That's me," Masters said as he moved toward the man. "You fellas are right on time." He unlocked the gate.

It took the two movers a couple of hours to unload the printing equipment into the space. Masters directed them so that each item was placed in the familiar configuration: printing press and work table in the middle of the room, light table, plate maker and portable darkroom in the rear.

The next morning Vukovich met Chance at the field of-fice. After signing out a G-car from the federal motor pool,

Vukovich steered onto the freeway and headed north toward Hollywood. Chance thumbed through a map book. Following his directions, Vukovich swung off the freeway at the Ventura Boulevard off-ramp and headed west on a commercial thoroughfare crowded with trendy shops and restaurants. They passed a health club, the roof of which balanced bronze-colored statues of a garishly muscular man and a woman holding hands.

"Turn left here," Chance said. They wound up a hill into a residential area made up of fashionable homes. Vukovich noted that though there were lots of Mercedes Benzes and Cadillacs parked in the driveways, lots of the places needed garden work. They watched addresses. Chance pointed at Rick Masters's sprawling home as they slowly cruised by.

Vukovich changed gears and steered up a steep hill onto a dead-end road which provided a clear side-view of Masters's place. They took turns with the binoculars. Vukovich guessed that the one-story stucco-and-wood home had at least four bedrooms. In the backyard a large, kidney-shaped swimming pool was nestled against the side of a hill. The pool had a flagstone island in its center and a young palm tree sprouted from the island.

Chance rustled through some paperwork in a plastic folder. "The intelligence file says he lives with a Mexican broad . . . a stripper. The owner of the club where she used to dance owed Masters for some hundreds he'd printed up. He couldn't pay so he gave Masters the broad as payment of the debt."

Nothing happened at the location for the next two hours. To kill time they talked office politics, discussing at length the rumor that Tom Bateman's wife had caught him with another woman during a weekend they'd spent at a Marriage Encounter retreat. That topic exhausted, Chance recounted some of the enormous restaurant tabs his real estate broker girlfriend had paid for with her expense account.

By noon they still hadn't seen Masters. The two agents

spoke briefly, then Vukovich started the engine and wound the car down the hill to Ventura Boulevard, pulling into the nearest service station. Chance leafed through the intelligence file until he found Masters's telephone number. He copied it on a scrap of paper and handed it to Vukovich. Vukovich walked to the telephone booth and dialed the number. A woman answered.

"Is Rick there?"

"Who's this?"

"John. I need to get in touch with Rick."

"He's out of town."

"When will he be back?"

"John who?" she said. "Who *is* this?"

"I'm a friend. Do you have a number where I can reach him?"

"We don't know no fucking John," she said angrily. The phone clicked; Vukovich returned to the car.

"He's out of town," he said as he started the engine. "That's all I could get out of her." He drove back to their surveillance location. A few minutes later a woman appeared at the kitchen window. She appeared to be standing in front of a sink washing dishes.

Chance focused the binoculars on her. "I'll be damned," he said, handing them to Vukovich. "I think that's the woman we saw at Waxman's office. The one driving the black Porsche."

Vukovich focused in. The woman wore a blue silk housecoat. "That's her all right," he said. "I wonder what she was doing at Waxman's office that night?"

"I doubt it's a coincidence that Rick Masters's girlfriend was the last one to see good ol' Max alive and breathing," Chance said.

"Waxman's book really did us a lot of good," Vukovich muttered under his breath.

"Whatsat?"

"The ledger book we snatched out of Waxman's office."

"What about it?"

"It hasn't helped. The book hasn't done us any good."

"It got the investigation rolling," Chance said diffidently.

Vukovich dropped the subject, and the two agents spent the next hour or so going over the details of Waxman's murder, though they'd rehashed it countless times before. For a change of pace they began to banter about how much they hated Tom Bateman. By three o'clock they were talked out.

The garage door of Masters's residence opened automatically. A silver Rolls-Royce backed out of the garage and into the street. The woman was driving; she proceeded down the hill.

"Let's see where she's going," Chance said.

Vukovich started the engine, put the car in gear and crept down the winding road after her. Taking care to remain far enough behind so that the G-car wouldn't be visible on the turns, they followed her to Coldwater Canyon Drive. There the Rolls made a right turn and headed south. At Ventura Boulevard she turned west into the commercial area. Less than a mile down the road, the Rolls slowed up and pulled into a parking lot next to a bank. To get a better view Vukovich swung a U-turn and pulled up across the street. The woman went into the bank.

Chance climbed out of the G-car and followed her in. He came out of the bank less than a minute later and was back in the passenger seat. "She went into the safe deposit box area," he said.

A few minutes later the woman left the bank carrying a small package. She got back in the Rolls and headed south toward the freeway. Staying well under the speed limit, she drove freeways and surface streets directly to Beverly Hills. Once there she entered a quiet neighborhood made up of wide streets lined with palm trees and palatial homes. The Rolls pulled into a circular driveway in front of a pillared, colonial-style mansion and parked. The woman got out of the Rolls holding the package and walked to the front door. She was knocking as Vukovich drove slowly by. The door was answered by a fiftyish, clean-featured man whose white hair was in curlers.

"It's Reggie Musgrave," Chance said as he noted the address of the place on a small tablet. "The owner of the Porsche she drove to Waxman's office."

"Father Donegan the Private Eye Priest," Vukovich said, recalling the name of the TV program Musgrave starred in. After the woman went inside the house Vukovich parked a good distance up the street.

Precisely twelve minutes later the front door opened. Vukovich grabbed the binoculars. Empty-handed, the woman headed for the Rolls-Royce. "She delivered," he said.

"What would a TV star want with counterfeit money?" Chance said as they watched her pull out and drive past them.

"Who knows?"

The surveillance log for the rest of the day read:

1359 hrs.　　Suspect depart 3021 Alta Vista Road, Beverly Hills

1410 hrs.　　Suspect arrive Mr. Edward Hair Salon, 1201 Rodeo Drive

1543 hrs.　　Suspect depart hair salon

1543 hrs.–1630 hrs.　　Suspect shopping along Rodeo Drive

1630 hrs.　　Suspect depart Rodeo Drive

1859 hrs.　　Suspect arrive Studio City residence

2400 hrs.　　Surveillance discontinued.

Vukovich felt edgy as well as exhausted after being cooped up in the car for sixteen hours. Chance sat slumped down in the passenger seat, his eyes closed as Vukovich drove through dark Studio City streets on his way back to the field office.

"Maybe the delivery was some kind of a legitimate deal," Chance said. "Maybe it's nothing."

"It had to be *something*. I say she was carrying. As soon as she left the bank she began driving slow. She was worried about getting pulled over by a cop."

"I wonder where Masters is?" Chance said, though he lacked the energy to speculate on this when his partner didn't answer.

They said little for the rest of the trip. At the Federal Building Vukovich drove into the darkness of the underground garage.

CHAPTER ELEVEN

By midnight the press was rolling, its train-like clatter reverberating off the cement floor and walls in the rented cubicle. Rick Masters picked up a rag and wiped green ink off his hands. He grabbed one of the 8″ × 11″ sheets as it snapped from under the sheet-transfer cylinder into the tray and held it up to a fluorescent light fixture hanging in the middle of the room. Using a jeweler's loupe, he examined the portrait of Andrew Jackson on each of the three images because he knew this was what the banks looked for first. The meshwork of vertical and horizontal lines which made up the background of the portrait was clear and distinct. *"All right,"* he said out loud.

It was 4 A.M. by the time he'd finished trimming the images of the bill to size with a large paper cutter. It wasn't till then that he realized he'd had nothing to eat or drink since he'd arrived there . . . he was beginning to feel light-headed.

After carefully wrapping and packing the trimmed twenties, he placed them in the suitcase. Then he painstakingly gathered up every scrap of paper in the cubicle and stuffed everything into a black plastic trash bag. Using a screwdriver, he removed the thin aluminum lithographic plate from the plate cylinder on the printing press. Using tiny snips he cut the plate into inch-sized pieces and tossed the pieces into the trash bag. He tied the bag securely with a piece of wire.

He phoned for a taxi, then made one final check in every corner of the plant. Satisfied that everything was in order, he left carrying the trash bag and suitcase, locked the door behind him. Masters tossed the trash bag into a brimming commercial trash receptacle that was next to the fence. As he waited for the taxi, he thought about the first time he'd printed counterfeit money. He'd rented a shop less than two blocks from the Los Angeles Federal Building where the treasury agents had their office. As the press had been rolling, he'd phoned their office and held the receiver next to the clacking press. Youthful horseplay.

The taxi arrived a few minutes later. The driver was a middle-aged man with red cheeks and thick glasses.

"Caesars Palace," Masters said as he climbed into the cab.

"You got it," the driver said. He had liquor on his breath. "What are ya doing out here in the middle of the night?" the driver asked as he made an extra-wide turn onto Las Vegas Boulevard.

"My car broke down."

The driver hiccuped. "Oh," he said, closing the matter.

At Caesars Palace, Masters went immediately to the registration desk, signed the register as Arthur Truman and headed directly for his room. After showering he turned on the television (a talk show featuring an actress talking about a book she'd written on reincarnation) and made himself comfortable on the bed. He awoke seven hours later in the same position. The television was tuned to a children's program.

Masters staggered from the bed and dialed room service. After eating a double breakfast, he changed clothes and, carrying the suitcase containing the counterfeit money, strolled along the corridor to the registration desk. He paid his room bill with a few of the phony twenties, then headed for the door. Before leaving, he stopped at a roulette wheel near the front door which was manned by a young female croupier with peroxide blonde hair. There was no one else at the table. As he set a phony twenty on the red, he felt a tightening in his loins. The woman spun the wheel. Red it was. She pushed two twenty dollar chips toward him. He picked them up and dropped them in his pocket. As he headed out the door and across the street to where he'd parked his car the day before, he felt satisfied; as emptied of energy as if he'd just screwed for three hours straight.

Masters drove the speed limit all the way back to Los Angeles.

The next day the agents were at the surveillance spot by 7 A.M. Nothing occurred the entire day. By the time Rick Masters drove into the driveway at eight-thirty that night, Vukovich's legs were sore from sitting. The lights in the house went out about midnight.

The next day was much of the same. Masters's only trip was to a Rolls-Royce dealer, where he waited as his car was serviced. He returned home without stopping anywhere else. Late that night, Vukovich checked his wristwatch. It was 11:53 P.M., as if the exact time mattered when nothing was happening.

"I wonder who they are?" Blanca said as she stood next to Masters at the darkened bedroom window.

"Feds, cops. What's the difference," Masters said, keeping his eyes on the vehicle parked on the hill above them. The outline of the sedan was barely illuminated by a street light. It looked like two men in the front seat.

"What are we gonna do?" Blanca said.

He sipped the drink he was holding and set it down on a

dresser table. He smiled. "Let's give 'em something to look at."

"Huh?"

Chance nudged Vukovich awake. "Look," he said.

Vukovich rubbed his eyes. Someone had turned on the floodlamps in Masters's backyard. The island in the middle of the swimming pool was illuminated like a spot on center stage. Vukovich sat up in the seat.

The back door of the house opened and closed. Two nude figures emerged, dove into the pool and swam to the island. They climbed up and got to their feet. It was Masters and his girlfriend. For the next few minutes, they sucked and fucked in various positions. Finally, they both turned and waved in the direction of the agents. Using the binoculars, Vukovich could tell they were both laughing. They dove back in the water, climbed out of the pool and returned to the house. The lights went off.

Neither man spoke as Vukovich started the engine and proceeded down the hill. He headed directly for the Angel's Flight.

The bar was smoky and crowded. The bartender was setting up drinks on a red-faced, newly promoted police sergeant sitting in a booth with three homely, fortyish women wearing nurse's uniforms. Chance and Vukovich slid into a booth behind them.

"We're at the same point everyone gets to with Rick Masters," Chance said after they were served. "Nowhere. He's too slick for a surveillance."

"So what do we do now?"

"Either hang up our jocks and admit he's untouchable or be slicker than he is," Chance said.

"Have anything in mind?"

"A wiretap on his phone would do the trick."

"To get a court order for a wiretap we'd have to swear out an affidavit explaining how we developed Masters as a suspect in the case," Vukovich said. "And Bateman reviews all wiretap paperwork. I'm sure he'd enjoy reading about the ledger book you stole from Waxman's office."

"The book that *we* stole." Chance corrected him.

"The point is that there is no way we can get a legal court order for a phone bug without mentioning Waxman's ledger."

Chance sipped his drink, winked at one of the nurses sitting in the booth. She winked back. "You're right," he said. "The only way to do it is to be resourceful."

"Resourceful?"

Chance looked his partner in the eye. "If *you* were a judge and knew what you and I know about Masters . . . that he is the biggest funny money dealer in town . . . would you authorize a wire on his phone?"

"Of course. You and I both knew the man is a counterfeiter."

"So let's say you're the judge. You give the go-ahead. We grab ourselves a nice hot-mike-and-receiver set-up and we're in business. We tune in on Tricky Ricky talking money talk to all of his asshole friends."

"What good would that do? Anything we heard him say would be inadmissible in court anyway."

"That's right, which is why we're not going to get authorization. We won't be listening to the man to find out that he's a counterfeiter. We already *know* that. We listen to find a weakness . . . an in to make a solid case on him some other way."

"You're talking about getting fired and possibly ending up in the joint if we got caught. You're talking about committing a felony."

"That is *if* we got caught," Chance said. He took a drink and wiped his mouth with the back of his hand.

"Where would we get the equipment?"

"There's a bug in the office safe," Chance said. "A hot mike. It was used on that last Colombian case and it hasn't been returned to headquarters yet. If we used it for a day or so before it was sent back, no one would be the wiser."

The bartender came to the table. He emptied the ashtray and set cocktail napkins which had a cartoon of a nude woman and a policeman cavorting in a cocktail glass under their drinks.

"Big fight here last night," he said in a hollow, smoker's voice. "Narco detective versus a vice cop. The argument had something to do with a broad. They fought like dogs . . . all the way out into the street." He chuckled. A man wearing a T-shirt at the other end of the bar waved an empty glass; the bartender rushed off.

"We can either sit here and talk about how nice it would be to arrest Masters," Chance said, ". . . or we can get off our asses and *do* something about it."

Vukovich said nothing for a while. "Risky as hell," he said finally.

With this Chance dropped the subject and recounted, without sparing any details, his recent seduction of a young woman who lived in the apartment next door to him. Vukovich half-listened as he thought about the wiretap. Finally, Chance finished his story.

One of the nurses dropped coins in the jukebox. It blared "You're in the Jailhouse Now." There were some whoops and hollers from around the bar, then a ripple of laughter.

The two partners had another drink and after more small talk Vukovich brought up the wiretap again.

"I'm not breaking into Masters's house to plant the bug," he said. "No matter how much planning goes into those operations, there's still too much risk. There's always the chance that some little old lady is going to be staring out her window right when we shim the door. She calls the cops and the story's been told. We end up getting booked. And for what? So Rick Masters has been printing and selling wholesale for the past ten years without getting caught? Hell, fifteen years ago Jim Hart caught him and he still only got three years' sentence. If the prosecutors and judges and all the greasy-palmed politicians and all the soap-opera-watching-morons that sit on juries don't care, why should we?''

"What if I told you I knew of a way to get the bug in the house without any risk?''

"Without any risk whatsoever?''

"*No* risk.''

"Then I'd probably go along with it,'' Vukovich said.

Because they were still going over the details of the plan when the bar closed, Vukovich and Chance were the last to leave.

The weather was overcast, gray, but the usual coastline fog had started to dissipate.

Jim Hart parked his G-car in the parking lot in front of the Terminal Island administration building. He checked his wristwatch; it was almost noon. To kill time, he fiddled with a small bag of trout flies which he'd picked up at a sporting goods store after signing in at the Field Office and checking out a car. He rolled down the window. The smell of the fish cannery filled the car like an invisible gas. He remembered an old-time counterfeiter once telling him that after his first stretch in Terminal Island, he'd never eaten fish again.

At precisely noon Manny Contreras, a fortyish, triangle-faced worm of a man with big ears, drooping mustache and a shaved head, pachuco-strutted out the front door of the prison. He wore bell-bottom denim trousers which covered the tops of his shoes and a long-sleeved beige sport shirt which was at least a size too large. Both sleeves and the collar of the shirt were buttoned in the manner of East L.A. barrio gang members. Under one arm he carried a package wrapped with brown paper and string, which Hart knew was the way a prisoner's personal property was stored until the day of his release.

Without so much as a glance at the parking lot, Manny

Contreras took loping strides toward the road that led toward the bus stop on Ferry street. Hart waited a while, then started the engine. He drove slowly out of the lot and pulled up next to the newly released prisoner. ''Wanna ride?'' he said.

Contreras stopped, squinted into the car. ''I remember you, man,'' he said in barrio dialect.

''Hop in,'' Hart said in a cheerful tone.

Manny Contreras looked around. He reached for the door handle as if it might be red hot. Hesitantly, he opened the door and climbed in.

Jim Hart stepped on the accelerator and headed toward the bridge. ''It's been a long time,'' he said.

''Two years, four months and twenty-three days,'' Contreras said. He held the package on his lap. ''What are you doing down here?''

''I just interviewed an inmate,'' Hart lied.

''You mean you interviewed a rat,'' Contreras said with a wry smile.

Hart shrugged as he steered across the bridge. The cannery smell dissipated. ''I've never looked down on a man who does what he thinks is right for himself and his family. People do what they have to do.''

Contreras glanced at him snidely. He set the package between them. ''Check this out. The only reason you Feds spent so much time making a case on me was because I was carrying for Rick Masters. You wanted me to be a snitch. So I guess you wasted your motherfucking time, man. Check it out.''

Hart shrugged. ''I guess we both wasted some time.''

''I ain't got no hard feelings, man. At least you didn't lie in court.''

''Thanks, Manny,'' Hart said.

''Check this out, man. You're the only cop I ever met who doesn't lie in court,'' Contreras said as he stared at cars passing by. ''Cops are born to lie.''

Hart noticed that there was lots of gray hair in Contreras's mustache: prison gray. Deep lines were etched around his eyes.

"That's the way they got my brother," Contreras said as he stared at the road. "Check this out. He had the funny money under the front seat of his car. They didn't have no probable cause to search the car, so they said they found the bundle in his shirt pocket. They lied, man."

"Who's they?"

"A Fed named Chance," Contreras said. "You ever heard of him?"

Hart shook his head. "Years ago it was legal to search a car," Hart said. "The Supreme Court changes its mind every few years. Funny."

"Check this out. My brother beat the case anyway. They forgot to warn him of his rights in Spanish so he beat the case. That's the funny part. He don't even speak Spanish." He chuckled.

"I almost didn't recognize you with your head shaved," Hart said.

"Check this out. I've shaved my head once a year since I was a kid. All the home boys do. It grows back in like real nice."

"Rick Masters has been doing real well in the past few years," Hart said.

Manny Contreras only smiled.

Hart drove the freeway north through Watts.

"Are you going near East L.A.?" Contreras said as they neared the downtown interchange.

"No trouble."

A few minutes later Hart swung off the freeway at Fourth Street. He passed Hollenbeck Park, a littered green patch that was referred to as the battlefield by the local precinct cops who answered gang fight calls there every week.

"How's your little sister?" Hart said.

"Check this out. She graduated from junior college, and now she's got a good job with the housing authority."

"I'm sure glad I was able to keep her out of the soup when you were arrested."

"Check this out. She was just with me. She didn't have no idea I was carrying the funny money."

"I'm glad I believed you and let her go. An arrest record might have kept her from getting that good job."

Contreras didn't respond to the remark. He stared ahead. "This is where I want to get out," he said finally.

Hart pulled the car to the curb.

Contreras turned to him. "Fuck all this cat-and-mouse shit, man. So what the fuck do you want from me?"

"I need a couple of questions answered."

"Check this out. I ain't answering no questions about any of my home boys. I ain't answering no questions about any of my people."

"I'm interested in a T.I. prisoner named Carmine Falcone. Do you know him?"

"Check this out. All the funny money people in T.I. know all the other funny money people."

"I want to know how close he is to Rick Masters."

"Close."

"How close?"

"Falcone is as close as anybody in the world is to that paranoid motherfucker. He helps with the printing. And after the bills are printed, he's the one who ages 'em to make 'em look used. He soaks 'em and dries 'em."

"What does Falcone talk about in the joint?"

"The same thing everyone else talks about: pussy. Check it out."

"What else?"

"Check this out. When he first came in, he told people he wasn't going to be there long. Like he had something fixed up or maybe an appeal bond or some shit like that. Now he don't talk about that no more. The word is that he found out he can't get out through the back door and he's going to have to do his time.'' Contreras spoke without making eye contact. He opened the car door and got out. "Check this out. I know it wasn't no accident that you were down there today,'' he said as he leaned down to window level.

Hart shrugged.

"You did me a favor by not arresting my sister,'' Contreras said. "So now we're even.''

"We're even,'' Hart said as Manny Contreras turned and strutted away.

He swung a U-turn on Fourth Street and headed back toward Terminal Island.

CHAPTER TWELVE

A musclebound black guard unlocked a steel door and led Hart down a corridor to a small room furnished with a wooden table and two chairs. Hart sat down. On the table was a styrofoam cup filled with ashes and cigarette butts.

A few minutes later the guard showed a dark-haired man of medium height and weight into the room. He wore prison denims and carried what looked like a medicine bottle in his left hand.

"Carmine Falcone?" Hart said.

The man nodded.

Hart offered him a chair. As he sat down, Hart noticed the label on the bottle: Pepto-Bismol. He nodded at it. "Stomach problems?"

"Ulcer," Falcone said as he touched his stomach with both hands. "They want me to have an operation, but I can't stand the thought of one of these prison butchers slicing me open. I'd rather drink Pepto-Bismol and shit pink cement. What's this all about?"

"Rick Masters."

"What about him?"

"I've been told that you know him."

"Who told you that?" Falcone said. As he spoke, Hart noticed a cakey residue of the medicine outlining his bluish, Mediterranean lips.

"I get paid to ask questions . . . not answer them."

"So I know Rick Masters."

"So I want to lock him up."

Carmine Falcone casually set the cylindrical bottle on its side. He spun the bottle and stopped it. "So what do you want from me?"

"I'm looking for some help."

"You're looking for me to rat him out for you. You're looking to make me into a snitch."

"Call it what you want," Hart said. "I'm looking for some help. I want to put the man away."

"I've taken four falls and never ratted on anyone in my life," Falcone said, staring at the medicine bottle. "And don't think I haven't had plenty of chances. I've been offered immunity from prosecution more times than I remember. But I've never testified. I've never set anyone up. When I take a fall I go to the joint alone. I do my time alone."

Because the small, unventilated room was warm Hart removed his coat and hung it on the back of his chair. "If Masters is your friend, I can't blame you for keeping quiet. I'd never hand up a friend either. Anyone who would is slime."

Falcone looked at Hart with a puzzled expression. He reached into his shirt pocket and took out a pack of Camels, tapped out a cigarette. He lit up and blew a sharp stream of smoke. "You heard that I'm on the outs with Rick. That's why you came here, isn't it? Well, just because I'm on the outs with somebody doesn't mean I'm willing to snitch 'em off. You gotta really hate someone to want to ship 'em to this place . . . you gotta hate their guts."

"I heard you hated Masters's guts."

"So maybe I do," Falcone said, focusing his attention on

the medicine bottle again. "But that still doesn't mean I'm going to roll over and play informer. It would take a lot more than that."

"What *would* it take?" Hart said after a moment.

Carmine licked his lips. He picked up the Pepto-Bismol, unscrewed the cap and took a big gulp. He replaced the cap. More of the pink substance outlined the corners of his mouth. "I'm down, man," he said. "I want to raise. I want out. I'd be crazy if I didn't want out." Falcone used the thumb and forefinger of his right hand to massage his forehead for a moment. "I've been passing and dealing bad paper since I was eighteen," he said quietly. "And do you know what I have to show for it? Nothing. Nothing but a motherfucking duodenal ulcer. D'ya know who I am? I'm the guy who's always five minutes late when the big score is taken down. I'm the one who's waiting outside the door when the big boys are doing the million dollar funny money deal. And when the cops come, I'm the first one to get busted. This is the story of my life. I shit you not." He spun the cap off the Pepto-Bismol bottle and drank again. "And now you're sitting here asking me to be a snitch. This is something I've never done. Ask anyone whose ever known me. I've never sucked a cock and I've never snitched."

"I understand there's been some bad blood between you and Rick."

"That's personal."

Hart scratched his head, then folded his hands on the table. "If you're willing to work for me, to help me put Masters away, I'm willing to talk to a judge about changing your sentence to a parole term. Are you interested?"

"What would I have to do?" Falcone said after a while. "Like *exactly*?"

"Answer all my questions about Masters and testify against him in open court."

"I'd rather stay in here for the rest of my life than testify in open court," Falcone said.

Hart sat silently for a moment. "Then I guess we can't do business."

Hart stood up and put on his jacket. "Sorry," he said, his tone passive. "If you change your mind just give me a ring." Hart left the room.

It was almost 8 P.M.

Vukovich sat alone at his desk in the field office, nervously doodling circles with a ballpoint pen. Chance, sitting at the desk next to him, made romantic small talk on the phone with one of his girlfriends.

At the end of the long series of desks Jack Kelly, a veteran special agent with the torso of a longshoreman, sat poring over a report. Finally, he stuffed the report in a drawer. After locking his desk he stood up and shrugged on a well-worn blue suit coat. "See you tomorrow, lads," he said as he walked past them.

Vukovich gave a wave. He breathed a sigh of relief.

"Gotta run, baby," Chance said to end his phone conversation. He set the receiver down. Chance quickly left the room and was back less than a minute later. "He was the last one. Everybody's gone," he said furtively. He motioned to Vukovich.

Vukovich followed him to Bateman's office and stood guard at the door as Chance rifled Bateman's desk. "Can't find it," Chance said after a few minutes. Standing with hands on hips, he surveyed the room.

"Maybe he keeps it on his key ring."

"No way," Chance said. "The manual says that tech-room keys can't leave the Field Office. And you know how he is about the manual." He stepped to a small credenza in the corner of the room and began searching. "It's got to be here somewhere." After completing his search of the credenza he moved to a four-drawer filing cabinet next to it. He searched drawers from the bottom up.

"Maybe we ought to just forget the whole thing," Vukovich said as he imagined Bateman bursting into the office and catching them.

Ignoring the remark, Chance peeked into each of the hanging flower pots in the office. "Bingo!" He held up a key attached to a plastic identification tag. Brushing by Vukovich, he hurried down the hall. He stopped at a door with a sign posted on it which read "Do not enter without signing log."

Chance slid the key into the lock, opened the door and stepped inside. He flipped on the light. Vukovich remained at the door. The walls of the room were lined with metal wall units and open cupboards laden with radio receivers and transmitters, battery packs, testing equipment, cameras and lenses of all varieties. On the opposite side of the room was a large green felt-covered workbench scattered with soldering irons, tube testers and other electronic miscellanea. Below the bench were labeled drawers. He pulled open the drawer labeled telephone hot mikes. He picked up a thin, round metal object the size of a telephone mouthpiece and shoved it into his pocket. From a shelf he removed a receiver which looked like a car radio. He hurried out of the room. After returning the key to Bateman's flower-pot hiding place, they left the office with the equipment.

Rick Masters woke early, as was his custom. Lying next to the nude Blanca in a state of semi-sleep, he heard birds fluttering about in the tree next to the bedroom window. He half considered what he would have for breakfast and whether he would wake Blanca for morning sex.

There was the sound of a car pulling up in the driveway. Brakes squealed. He jumped out of bed and pulled back the curtain. Plain-clothes cops with badges pinned to their suit coats piled out of the car and ran toward the house. Another car pulled up at the curb. More cops.

Blanca sat up in bed. "What's wrong?"

"Cops!" he said as he snatched up the envelope containing samples of the newly printed twenties, rushed into the bathroom. Frantically, he tore the small stack of bills in half and tossed the pieces into the toilet. He turned the flush handle.

Violent knocks on the front door.

"Police with a search warrant! Open the door or we'll kick it in!"

Blanca ran into the bathroom and emptied a glassine envelope containing cocaine into the swirling bowl.

"Is that *everything*?" he said.

"I think so," she said. There was fear in her eyes. Grabbing her by the arm, he pulled her out of the bathroom and closed the door behind him.

There were terrific blows to the front door. The sound of the door jamb splitting, people running in the house. Detectives pointing guns vaulted into the bedroom. "Hands up! Hands up!"

Masters and Blanca complied. One of the raiders rushed past them to the bathroom. They were allowed to dress after one of the officers checked each piece of clothing for weapons. Their hands were handcuffed behind them and they were ushered into the living room.

Detectives began pulling out kitchen drawers and emptying them on the floor.

"My name is Lindberg," said a tall man standing in the middle of the room holding a clipboard under his arm. "L.A.P.D. Robbery-Homicide. You're both under arrest for murder."

"The murder of who?" Masters said.

"Max Waxman," he said as if reading a train schedule.

"I'd like to phone my attorney," Masters said.

"I want a lawyer," Blanca chimed.

The cop smiled. "What'd ya flush down the toilet?"

* * *

Vukovich hugged the steering wheel in the G-car, maintained his gaze on Masters's house. Chance tuned the commercial radio to a country-and-western station.

"They've been in there for almost two hours," Chance said.

As he said this a rotund, bald detective with a mustache ushered Masters and his girlfriend out of the front door to a waiting police car. He opened the rear door and motioned the prisoners in. Another detective came out of the house and climbed in the driver's seat. The car drove off.

Vukovich put the G-car in gear and steered down the street to Masters's place, parking it in front. Chance opened the glove compartment and took out the hot mike. He shoved it in his shirt pocket. Together they headed inside. The place was a shambles. The living room carpet had been ripped away from its tacking; the sofa and chairs were overturned. Lindberg stood at the sofa holding a cushion in his hands.

"Come up with anything?" Chance asked.

"Nary a fucking thing," Lindberg said as he ripped the sofa cushion open and peered inside.

"Mind if we scout around a little?" Chance said.

"Help yourself," the detective said. "It's the least we can do since you provided the probable cause for the search warrant." He picked up another cushion and tore it apart.

Vukovich noticed a telephone on the coffee table. He and Chance milled about, poking at items here and there in the living room. After a while they toured the rooms in the house. Finally they returned to the living room. Lindberg had moved into the kitchen area with another detective.

Chance knelt down next to the coffee table. As Vukovich kept watch, he lifted the handset off the phone cradle, unscrewed the mouthpiece and removed the speaker. Without hesitation he replaced it with the hot mike, screwed the mouthpiece back on and set the receiver back on the cradle.

As he stood up he shoved the phone speaker into his pants pocket.

Lindberg stepped back into the room. "We're about ready to lock the place up," he said.

"Are you going to be able to file murder charges?"

"Not a chance," Lindberg said. "The problem is that Waxman's wounds were mortal. So even though you saw Masters's girlfriend show up at Waxman's office a couple of hours before his death, the autopsy showed that Waxman couldn't have lived for more than a few minutes with the nature of his wounds. So the woman couldn't have done it."

"Did you check out the Porsche she arrived in?" Chance said.

"That's a dead end also. I talked to an actor named Reggie Musgrave, the owner of the car. He reported the car stolen from the studio lot the night of the murder."

"What kind of a guy is he?" Chance said.

"Typical Hollywood three-dollar bill."

"Did you find anything in the house that ties Masters to Waxman?" Chance said.

"Nope. And no weapons. *And* neither he nor his lady are going to answer any questions. They both asked for a lawyer right off the bat. We'll sweat 'em for a couple of hours anyway, but we'll have to let 'em go."

"Too bad."

"Yeah, it breaks my heart to think that someone got away with murdering poor old Max." He feigned a sorrowful look. "He'll be sorely missed in our fair city."

The detective in the kitchen laughed at the remark.

CHAPTER THIRTEEN

Rick Masters stood in front of a high, steel-reinforced counter in the L.A. county jail. A pale and sleepy-eyed sheriff's deputy shoved a printed form across the counter in a well-practiced motion. Masters used a pen attached to a thin chain to sign the form. The deputy compared the signature to another printed form which was stapled to a clear plastic bag containing Masters's personal property. He tossed the bag. Masters caught it as it hit his chest. The deputy pointed to the door. As Masters moved toward it, a hydraulic lock snapped. Masters pulled the door open and stepped outside to face the dead-end street at the rear of the jail. It was dusk and slightly chilly. He glanced at his wristwatch in the property bag. He'd been in jail exactly forty-nine hours.

A limousine pulled up at the curb. The driver climbed out and opened the rear door on the street side. Masters climbed in back with Grimes. "What took you so long?" he said.

"It couldn't have been done any faster. Take my word for it. I just came from the judge's chambers. And I'm talking about the *senior* judge of the Superior Court. I had to do a lot of fast talk . . ."

"Where's Blanca?" Masters interrupted.

"One of my investigators went to pick her up at the women's jail. She'll probably be home before you."

The driver made a U-turn. He cruised slowly past the five-story cement structure which Masters knew, because a prisoner had told him, was the biggest jail in the free world.

"Why did I get arrested?" Masters said.

"I see it as a harassment thing. They searched your house and couldn't find anything. They probably arrested you because they were pissed off. They knew they couldn't keep you for more than a day or two."

"That's the way I read it too. The only part I don't understand is how they got the search warrant for my house. Where did their information come from?"

"The Feds were watching Waxman's place when he was hit. They saw Blanca go there shortly before Max got it."

Masters said nothing. His stomach tightened. He rubbed his chin. "How do you know?"

"It's right in the affidavit for the search warrant. It says that Treasury agents had the place under surveillance."

"Shit."

Grimes gave him a look of concern. "Is there anything I should know at this point? I'm asking as your attorney."

"Where were they watching from?"

"The affidavit said they were watching from a church across the street."

Masters's mind quickly retraced his steps. He almost breathed a sigh of relief as he realized that he'd been nowhere near the Wilshire Boulevard entrance to the law office on the night of the murder.

"You seem concerned," Grimes said. "If there's something I should know, I'd rather hear it sooner than later. I remind you that I'm your lawyer and anything you say to me is privileged."

Ignoring the question, Masters leaned back in the seat and

closed his eyes. The traffic was heavy on the way to his house.

Inside the motel room, John Vukovich stood at the window. Holding the foot-long aerial in his right hand, he moved it slowly along the window sill.

There was the sound of static as the transmitter finally came to life.

"Got it," Chance said as he sat at the dresser table in front of the receiver. Using a metal clip that was fastened to the base of the aerial, Vukovich attached the device to the lip of the windowsill. As he did this, he noticed for the first time that there was the faint odor of disinfectant in the room.

The window provided a partial view of a constantly busy Ventura Boulevard. Across the street was a private health club called the Studio City Adam and Eve Fitness Center. On the roof was a signboard with male and female silhouettes flexing on either side of lettering which read *Co-ed Jazzercise Classes—Join now*. To the right of the building was a franchise coffee shop advertised by a blinking neon hamburger sign on a twenty-foot pole; to the left, a self-service gas station whose sole attendant was locked in a glass booth for security.

Chance turned up the volume.

As the machine crackled to life, Masters's girlfriend could be heard hissing obscenities to the accompaniment of what sounded like furniture being moved around and drawers being slammed shut. This went on for a long time.

The sound of footsteps.

"Where are you going?" Blanca said.

"I have some errands to take care of," Masters answered. "I'll be back late tonight."

"And you're going to leave me here to clean up after the pigs?"

"I guess you could say that." A door opened and closed.

Vukovich wandered to the other side of the room and joined Chance at the radio.

"Funny feeling, isn't it?" Chance said as he adjusted dials.

"Whatsat?"

"Committing a felony."

"I guess you could say that."

"What makes it especially funny is that we're doing nothing more than what cops did for many long years. Hell, the prisons used to be filled with hoods who'd been caught with wiretaps."

"Hart told me that years ago every agency in town had taps going. The P.D., D.A.'s office, FBI."

"It's the system. You either break the rules or you can't do your job. It would have taken us a month to go through the maze of chickenshit legal procedure to get a legal wiretap."

The sound of Blanca straightening up went on for about two more hours, then the telephone rang. The receiver was picked up, causing a loud buzz sound.

"Hello," Blanca said. Chance adjusted the volume because of the static. It didn't help. The conversation was barely decipherable.

"Is Rick home?" a man said.

"He went to do some errands."

"When will he be back?"

"Late."

"I'm coming over."

"What if he comes back early?"

"I won't stay long."

Because of increased static, the rest of the conversation was indecipherable.

The phone receiver clicked and the static stopped.

"Whataya make of that?" Vukovich said.

"Sounds like she's got a boyfriend."

More cleaning up sounds. As the woman worked she

hummed a tune. About an hour later, the doorbell rang. Footsteps. The door opened. The murmur of voices. The sound of footsteps which became louder and then diminished. Silence.

"They must have passed by the mike and into the bedroom," Vukovich said.

Approximately thirty minutes later the transmitter came to life again with the distant sound of voices. Footsteps came closer to the microphone and stopped. Wet kisses. "I love you, baby," Blanca said. More kisses.

"Gotta run," the man's voice. Footsteps. A door opening. The sounds were distant. Chance turned up the volume.

"I wonder who it was?" Vukovich said.

"Somebody who stopped by for a quickie."

The visit was the only interesting event of the day. The rest of the day consisted of more cleaning up and a few inconsequential phone calls. About 6 P.M. there was the sound of movement on the sofa nearest the telephone bug and after a while, the sound of breathing. Blanca's nap lasted almost an hour. The television was switched on. There were the usual TV sounds: news readers making happy talk, car chases, canned laughter interspersed with commercials. To relieve boredom Vukovich kept the motel television set tuned to the same channel as Blanca's.

Shortly after 11 P.M. there was the sound of a door being unlocked.

"Rick?" Blanca said.

"It's me."

The door opened. Footsteps. "Anyone call?" he said.

"No."

"Anyone come over?"

"No."

"Reggie was supposed to call today. He owes me for that pound you delivered."

"You know how he is," she said. "He probably got high and just forgot."

The sound of the telephone receiver being picked up. Dialing. Static. A man said hello.

"Rick here. How did you like it?"

"I love it."

"Where's my money?"

"Sorry I haven't gotten to you sooner. Been shooting at the studio twelve hours a day. Can you stop by tomorrow? Say about noon?"

"See you then," Masters said.

"Do you have any more?"

"How much are you interested in?"

"I'll take another one if you have it."

"Same place?"

"I'll leave the car doors unlocked. Leave it right in the glove compartment."

"That should be no problem," Masters said. The phone clicked.

"He wants another pound. He'll be at his place at noon. Take him the pound and collect what he owes me. Change cars on the way over. The cops might be still watching us. If everything doesn't look exactly right, just pass right on by. Be sure and keep the coke in a *briefcase* in the trunk of the car. Grimes says that the latest case law says that even if the cops have a search warrant for the car, they don't have the right to search a closed briefcase inside the car."

"Are you hungry?" she said.

"I've eaten."

"Did you go out with another woman tonight?"

"Why do you ask?"

"Just to make conversation."

"What if I said I did?"

"Then I guess I'd say I hope you had fun." There was anger in her voice.

The next half hour or so consisted of the distant sound of faucets being turned off and on, toilets flushing. Finally, there was silence.

"They went to bed," Vukovich said.

Chance stood up, flicked the receiver's power switch off. "Reggie Musgrave must be very tight with Masters," he said. "Masters used his car in a murder. He lets his woman deliver dope right to his house."

Vukovich nodded. He checked his wristwatch. "We just wasted sixteen boring hours sitting in a motel room to learn something we already knew."

"Not wasted," Chance said. "Now we know that Masters has a friend, a buyer." He strolled to the window and pulled the blind. Across the street the neon hamburger stopped blinking.

"Now what?" Vukovich said.

"Now we pay a visit to Reggie Musgrave."

"What about the hot mike? How do we get it back into the tech room?"

"We put it in. I guess we have to take it out."

CHAPTER FOURTEEN

Carmine Falcone slid his tray along the chow line. He nodded at an aluminum warming tray filled with scrambled eggs that were slightly off-color. The server, a balding, effeminate young man with plucked eyebrows and manicured nails, scooped a serving spoon of the eggs from the pan and dumped them onto his tray. As he did this, he leaned forward slightly. "There's something out on you. Be careful," he muttered.

"Who is it?" Falcone muttered back.

"The Dudes. It's a contract from the outside. That's all I know." The server slapped eggs on the next tray.

Falcone moved to a coffee maker. As he filled a coffee cup, he surveyed the area where the black prisoners usually sat. No one seemed to be looking at him. Nevertheless, he moved to the corner of the room and sat with his back to the wall. He suddenly didn't feel like eating and sat pushing the food around on his plate as he kept his eye on whoever moved near him. After an appropriate period of time he stood up and walked to the doorway. He dumped his breakfast into a trash can and bussed his tray, then stepped out of the chow hall and onto the brown grass of the exercise yard.

There was something wrong.

Instead of huddling together near the baseball diamond as they usually did, the black prisoners were roaming about either alone or in small groups. Staying close to the wall of the chow hall, Falcone mixed into a group of white prisoners. "What's up?" he said to a crew-cut older man whom he knew was a forger.

"I think the blacks are getting ready to clip somebody," he said out of the side of his mouth. "Lotta movement."

Two prisoners whom Falcone happened to be standing close to moved away from him quickly. The forger noticed this and his eyes became wide. He turned and hurried toward the main dormitory.

Falcone was alone. At the edge of a crowd of prisoners, four black men moved separately in his direction. He hurried back toward the chow hall. The blacks moved quickly into his path. Falcone turned and broke into a run straight toward the guard tower in the corner of the yard. He screamed and waved his hands frantically at the tower. The guard stepped from the booth with a rifle at port arm. The blacks backed off and disappeared into the crowd. A goon squad of husky guards hurried out of the administration building and went over to him. "I want protective custody," he said.

"What's wrong, Falcone? Didn't you pay your dues to the N.A.A.C.P.?" said one of the guards as they hurried him out of the yard.

Hart was sitting in an interview room. Falcone walked in and sat down to face him across the table. His Pepto-Bismol bottle hung heavily in the breast pocket of his light-green prison pajamas. He removed the Pepto-Bismol bottle from his pocket and set it on the table between them.

"Did the warden fill you in on what happened?" Falcone said.

"He phoned me and said that you wanted to be interviewed."

"And that I was in solitary at my own request?"

"Yes," Hart said as he looked the other man in the eye. "He told me that. He said that you were in a little trouble."

"Rick Masters has paper out on me. There's a price on my head so I asked to be put in protective custody. It's my right as a prisoner."

"Does that mean you'll testify for me?"

"I'll do something better than that. I'll help you catch Masters right in the act; when he's got the money coming off the press. How does that sound?"

"You can do that while in prison?"

"Of course not. You'll have to get me out. I need to raise in order to pull it off."

"And if I get you out and you don't keep your promise?"

"Then you can handcuff me and drive my ass right back down here to Fish City. You have nothing to lose."

"To get you out I'd have to convince a judge to sign a writ. I'd have to have something more than your promise. He'll ask me for your written statement about your involvement with Masters. Something to show your good faith."

Falcone lit a cigarette, coughed smoke. "I could be forced to testify to such a statement in court. And it's like I told you, I ain't going to take the stand. Masters or not, I've got my reputation to think about. It's not that I don't trust you as a person."

"If you won't swear out a statement, then how about just telling me about Masters. Give me some dates and some places on where you printed . . . a general rundown."

Falcone looked at the cigarette he was holding, then at Hart. "Right now I'm down and the jigs are after me. I need to raise to stay alive. But I'm not going to give you or anybody else the story until I set foot outside. I have no other way of insuring that I'm not being double-crossed."

"The judge will want something on paper."

Falcone leaned back in the chair. He smiled broadly. "My guess is that if you didn't think you had the juice to get me out, you wouldn't be sitting here."

"Don't be too sure."

"How's Dick Chance?" the young court clerk said as she led Hart down a wood-paneled court room hallway the next morning. She wore a light brown skirt and sweater which contrasted nicely with her flowing red hair.

"Uh, just fine," Hart said as he admired her hip-swinging gait.

She stopped in front of a door; the gold lettering on it read, Chambers of Judge Irving P. Malcolm—Private. "When you see Dick, tell him Cindy says hello," the woman said as she opened the door.

"I'll do that."

"The judge has only ten minutes before court reconvenes," she whispered as he stepped past her into the spacious office.

The judge, a florid-faced man with yellowish hair that needed combing, sat in a high-backed leather chair behind an oversized, polished wooden desk. The walls in the room were covered with rows of law volumes and the dark blue carpeting was soft, thick. The sound of classical music emanated faintly from a speaker box.

"What do *you* want?" the judge said without looking up from a law book.

Carefully, Hart set the document he was carrying on the desk. "I have a writ I'd like you to sign," he said.

"What kind of a writ?" the judge said as he thumbed more pages.

"It's a writ which releases a prisoner from Terminal Island so he can assist me on a counterfeiting case."

"Must be a pretty big case."

"Yes, your honor, it is," Hart said. "The target of the investigation is a major counterfeiter. . . ."

"I never sign such writs," the judge interrupted. He leaned closer to the law book and read in silence for what must have been fully three or four minutes. He picked up a pencil and made notes on a yellow pad. He set the pencil down and looked up. "Why are you still here?"

"I just spent all afternoon working on the wording of the writ. I'd really appreciate it if you would be kind enough to take a look at it."

Judge Malcolm let out his breath. He picked up the writ and thumbed through it perfunctorily. "Okay," he said. "Now I've looked at it." He tossed it forward on the desk.

"If you have any questions about it I'd be happy to try and answer them for you."

"I just sentenced Falcone to prison," Judge Malcolm said. "Why should I sign the paperwork to release him to your custody?"

"I need him to assist me in an investigation. I'll assume the full responsibility of getting him back to prison if he doesn't fulfill his promises."

"A bag of worms," the judge said. "Such writs are a great big bag of worms. I've been through this with agents before. I don't need the headache." He thumbed through more pages of the law book.

Hart stared at the writ for a moment. Hesitating, he picked it up. "Falcone is an associate of Rick Masters, a major organized crime figure. He prints everything from money to passports and has been getting away with it for years. I need to get Falcone out because I can't catch Masters any other way."

"That doesn't change the fact that Falcone is a sentenced federal prisoner," Malcolm said, looking up from the book. "The answer is no. I'm sorry, but the answer is no."

Suddenly Hart's face and hands felt warm. He folded the writ and shoved it in his coat pocket. He turned and moved toward the door.

"I realize that the law is sometimes hard to swallow,"

Judge Malcolm said in a condescending manner, ''but that's the system.''

Hart stopped, turned around to face the judge. ''What system?'' he said as he strained to modulate the anger in his voice.

''Don't say something you'll later regret,'' Malcolm said.

''I'm going to retire. This is my last chance at Rick Masters. I need Falcone on the street.''

The judge made an I'm-not-a-such-a-bad-guy smile. ''All crooks get caught eventually,'' he said. ''If not now, then later. You should know that.''

''That's where you're wrong,'' Hart said. ''Only the small fry, the passers, the bag-men get caught. The big boys just sit back and pull strings for a living.''

Malcolm frowned. ''I'm bound by the law,'' he said. ''I can't do favors.''

''If I was one of your ambulance-chasing cronies or some cookie-pushing public defender, I'll bet you'd be spread eagled on your desk right now trying to do me a favor. That's the *system*.''

The judge glared. ''Has it occurred to you that once Falcone is released he could just walk away?'' he said, his tone sarcastic. ''That his offer to cooperate could just be a ploy to escape?''

''I've talked with him and I think he's telling the truth.''

''And I suppose you're an expert on people telling the truth?''

''I'll bet I'm better at it than you are.''

Judge Malcolm leaned forward and pointed a finger at Hart. ''You're getting dangerously close to being rude,'' he said. ''I'm sure you'd prefer I not write a letter to your agent-in-charge reporting rudeness to a federal district judge.''

''There's nothing they can do to me when I'm this close to retirement.''

The judge's face turned red. Angrily, he stuck out his hand, palm up. "Let me look at the writ again."

Hart stepped forward, offered the document with his out-stretched hand. The judge yanked it away from him and looked through it again. He grabbed a fountain pen out of a desk holder, then scribbled his signature on the last page. "If anything happens it'll be your responsibility. I hold you personally accountable. If the prisoner escapes from custody, I will make an issue out of the incident. I'll make you testify in open court about how Falcone made a fool out of a veteran Treasury agent. You'll be humiliated." He tossed the writ across the desk to Hart. *"Do you understand what I'm saying?"*

"Yes, your honor," Hart said. "I'm sorry I said. . . ."

"Get the hell out of here," he said as he returned to his paperwork.

Hart hurried out of the room. After filing a copy of the writ at the U.S. court clerk's office, he drove straight to Terminal Island.

Vukovich made a pass by Masters's house. It was 9 P.M. and there were no lights on in the place.

"Head for a phone," Chance said with a tone of urgency. Vukovich steered down the hill to the Studio City business area. He pulled into the parking lot of a coffee shop. Chance climbed out of the car and ran to a telephone booth near the entrance. He returned quickly. "There's no answer. I say we do it now."

Vukovich pulled back into traffic and headed back toward Masters's house. "What if he's home and just not answering the telephone?"

"The lights are off. No one answers the phone. The man's not home, okay?"

"But he might come back any minute."

"Let's don't make this any harder than it is. Tomorrow is the weekly equipment inventory. If they find that hot mike missing from the tech room every agent in the office will go on the lie box and be asked about it. Everyone will pass except you and me. We have to get the mike. There's no other choice.''

Vukovich swallowed hard as he parked around the corner below the house. He turned off the lights and the engine. Taking care not to make noise to arouse any of Masters's neighbors, they took a screwdriver from the G-car's trunk and moved quietly up the street and around the corner.

Chance knocked softly on Masters's front door. There was no answer. As Vukovich watched the street, he used a screwdriver to try to shim the door.

''Can't do it,'' Chance said after what seemed like a long time. He moved past Vukovich and headed for the side of the house. In the dark, he crawled over a locked gate which led into the backyard. Vukovich followed. At the back door he used the screwdriver again. The door opened easily. Vukovich followed Chance in through the kitchen into the living room. Using a penlight for illumination, he quickly removed the hot mike from the telephone mouthpiece and replaced it with the standard mouthpiece he'd removed earlier.

There was the unmistakable sound of a blaring police radio in front of the house. Vukovich rushed to the front window and peeked out the curtain. *''Cops.''*

They rushed through the kitchen and out the rear door. At a full run they made it across the yard to a plant-covered incline which led down into an adjoining backyard. They stumbled frantically down the hill and shot across the backyard. After hopping a fence into another yard, Vukovich felt Chance grab him roughly by the shoulder.

''Wait,'' he said as he caught his breath. They peeked over the fence they'd just vaulted. Above them, there were flashlights surveying Masters's backyard.

Vukovich felt his heart trying to pound its way out of his chest. He was in the jungle again. . . .

The flashlights seemed to move to the opposite side of Masters's yard, away from them. "*Now*," Chance said. They ran between some houses and onto the street below. They scrambled into the G-car, Vukovich released the gear and allowed the sedan to coast down the hill until they were out of sound of the immediate area. He started the engine and sped around the corner. As they drove down Coldwater Canyon Drive two police cars rushed passed them going the other way. They returned to the empty Field Office and replaced the equipment in the tech room. Neither relaxed until they pulled up in the parking lot at the Angel's Flight.

Inside, Vukovich noticed that he was breathing hard even after the third drink.

"If we would have been caught, it would have been the end of everything," Vukovich said as Chance rambled on about the incident.

Chance slugged him on the shoulder. "Relax, partner. Relax. This is all part of it." He laughed.

"Part of what?"

Chance didn't hear him because he'd moved over one stool and put his arm around a blonde wearing a tight turtle-neck sweater.

Vukovich didn't get to sleep easily that night.

The next morning sitting at his desk, Vukovich was still mulling over the events of the previous night. Finally, he stood up and headed down the hallway to Bateman's office.

CHAPTER FIFTEEN

Bateman motioned him in the door and offered him a seat.

"You look a little hung over," Bateman said. He flashed his usual insincere grin, a favorite imitation of office comedians.

Vukovich nodded humbly.

"Of course I guess every good agent is entitled to a few drinks now and then," Bateman said.

"Have you made a final decision on who my permanent partner is going to be?" Vukovich asked.

"You must be a mind reader," Bateman said, maintaining his grin. "I was just going to call you in and tell you." He cleared his throat. "I've decided to leave you with Chance. You'll work with him from now on. I take it that meets with your approval?"

"Do I have any choice in the matter?" Vukovich said.

"Is there someone else you'd prefer as a partner?" Bateman asked. He tapped a pencil on his desk.

"I'd like to work with Jim Hart."

"I'm afraid that's impossible," Bateman said. "I don't like to waste fresh talent by putting it with someone who is basically retired-on-the-job. I know old salts like Hart are appealing to you younger men, but *job burnout* is infectious. Totally infectious.''

Vukovich nodded. He felt his face flush with anger.

"Of course, on the other hand, you're certainly welcome to fill out a form nineteen on Chance listing the reasons why you'd rather not work with him. Your input would be strictly confidential. Totally.''

"That's not true and you know it," Vukovich said.

"I guess the relevant question then is, do you intend to refuse to work with Chance permanently and if so, how do you intend to structure your refusal?''

"I'm not going to refuse," Vukovich said, straining to keep anger from his voice. "I'm just telling you that if I have a choice, I'd prefer to work with Hart.''

"Why?" Bateman said. "Certainly there must be some reason that you don't want to work with Chance . . . like working with him is either *viable* or it is *not viable*. I can fill out the form nineteen for you if you'd like. Chance would never have to see it.''

"Forget it," Vukovich said. He stood up.

"Up to you," Bateman said, gesturing as if it were out of his hands.

Vukovich walked out of the room and down the hallway to a locator board. Hart was signed out for lunch. He took the elevator to the ground floor and made the five-minute walk down First Street to Serge's restaurant where he knew Jim Hart usually ate.

The tiny stucco structure was situated between a beer bar and a mom and pop market on the area of First Street that led to the dry bed of cement known as the L.A. River. He opened the screen door and went inside. Hart sat at an oilcloth-covered table near a dirty bay window decorated with a hanging basket of wax fruit. He was reading a newspaper.

"I need some advice," Vukovich said as he sat down.

"Shoot."

As Vukovich recounted the details of his meeting with Bateman, Jim Hart nodded now and then. Carefully, he folded the newspaper.

"First of all," Hart said, "he'd never let a new agent like yourself work with me. He loses control that way. Asking you to fill out a form nineteen is typical Bateman. Anything to build a case on Chance. The only part I don't understand is why he won't give you a new partner. It doesn't make sense."

"When he questioned me about the arrest we made a few days ago I talked back to him," Vukovich said.

Hart nodded. "He can't stand to be put down. He takes it personal." He sipped his coffee and stared into the cup. "What is Chance up to?" he said calmly.

"He cuts corners," Vukovich said after pausing for a moment.

"What kinds of corners?"

"He's not on the take. I don't mean that."

"Then you mean he's cutting corners to gather evidence . . . to make cases? He's violating the good old exclusionary rule?"

Vukovich nodded.

"Every cop in the country does the same thing," Hart said. "Funny, isn't it, that the rules of evidence are based on technique rather than truth?"

"Chance goes too far," Vukovich said.

"I say no case is worth it. Who really cares about making cases?"

"If you really don't care, then what's your reason for coming to work every day?"

"To collect a paycheck," Hart said softly, not unlike a patient schoolteacher describing a mathematical procedure or perhaps the danger of fire. "Never forget that. No case is worth going to jail or losing your retirement. It's as simple as that."

Vukovich sat silently, mulling over Hart's advice.

"If Chance gets caught . . . uh . . . *cutting corners*, do you think he'll be a stand-up guy and take his medicine without involving you?" Hart asked.

"I think he would."

Hart lifted his eyebrows. "I think he just might hand you up on a silver platter."

"What makes you say that?"

"There been a lot of hot-dogs like Chance come through the office over the years. They always have the highest arrest stats and seem to go one of two routes: they either get promoted or fired. And the ones who get promoted eventually quit for higher-paying jobs. They never make retirement."

"That's all well and good, but . . ."

Hart held up a finger, smiled warmly. "I'm not finished."

"Sorry."

"What I was going to say is that all of the Chance types have one common denominator."

"What's that?"

"They all rat. Each and every one of them turns snitch when the going gets a little rough. And they don't care who they take down with them. It's the way they are."

"Chance would never rat me out. No way."

"There's only one way to find out," Hart said. "And by then it'll be too late."

"Then what do you suggest I do?"

"Get away from him."

"How?"

"You could fill out a form nineteen requesting a new partner."

"And make an enemy out of Chance."

"And that's not the half of it," Hart said. "Since Bateman hates Chance, he'll load up the comments section of the form with innuendoes about Chance's integrity. This will trigger a headquarters inspection. They'll make both of you account for every minute on your daily reports.''

''I can't do that,'' Vukovich said.

''The other alternative is to request a transfer.''

Vukovich rested his head on his hands, rubbed his eyes. ''What would you do?'' he said, finally looking up.

''Request a transfer.''

A hefty, middle-aged Mexican woman wearing an apron over a puffed-sleeved dress came out of the kitchen carrying a coffee pot. She refilled Hart's cup and asked Vukovich if he wanted to order. He shook his head no. She went to another table.

Hart poured cream in the coffee and took a sip. ''Great coffee here,'' he said. ''And the best Mexican food in town. Are you sure you're not hungry?''

Hart's words seemed to be emanating from a distance. Vukovich found himself staring out the window at the taco stand across the street. Two picnic tables were placed under its overhang.

''Years ago that taco stand was a heroin drop-off point for the Abel Vasquez organization,'' Hart said. ''A thousand deals must have taken place at those tables. I knew a fed narc that spent years trying to crack the Vasquez organization . . . all he ever talked about. It got to the point that on his days off you could find him staked out on one of the dealers. He probably spent more time around that taco stand than the owner. He finally arrested Abel Vasquez himself. That's what did him in.''

''Did him in?''

''He arrested Abel in a car and found some junk in the glove compartment. Because he didn't have probable cause to search the car, he testified in court that he'd seen Abel throw the dope out the driver's window just before he made the arrest. One of the other narcs on the arrest team was a rat. He got in a jam and told the U.S. attorney about how they'd falsified the evidence. Five narcs ended up in

Leavenworth over the incident, including the one who was the rat. The U.S. attorney double-crossed him on an immunity-for-testimony deal.''

Vukovich shook his head in dismay.

''Vasquez owns that taco stand now, along with three used-car dealerships and a hundred-room hotel in San Diego; a real dope-pushing success story . . . are you sure you don't want anything to eat?''

Vukovich shook his head as he continued to stare out the window. He watched a young woman in a sundress with a spiderweb tattoo covering her upper arm push a baby carriage past the window.

''Sometimes I wish I'd have stayed in the army,'' Vukovich said. ''Thanks for the advice.'' Slowly, he got up and left the restaurant.

The weather was clear and warm and there was a breeze, strong and cool, coming from the harbor. It was midday and commercial fishing boats could be seen heading in from past the breakwater.

Jim Hart wandered around in front of the Terminal Island prison administration building to kill time. Most of the sad-looking visitors, mostly women, who passed through the heavy doors of the building gave him disdainful looks—probably, he thought, because they could tell he was some kind of cop. Hart checked his wristwatch. It had been two hours since he'd presented the court order to the assistant warden, an overweight black man who'd perfunctorily leafed through the document, then told Hart he didn't know how long it would take to process Falcone out because he was short-handed. Hart absentmindedly wound the wristwatch his wife had given him as a birthday present years ago.

Finally, Falcone came through the doors. He was dressed in a wrinkled Hawaiian shirt and levis and wore blue running shoes. He carried a small brown package tied with white string.

"You're a man of your word, I'll say that," he said to Hart. They shook hands.

Hart nodded toward his G-car and Falcone followed. "I want you to understand something," Hart said, once they were in the car. "I got you out because you told me you could help me set Masters up. I've kept my part of the bargain and I expect you to keep yours. If you double-cross me and split, I will dedicate my life to finding you. And when I do, not only will I beat the shit out of you and put you back in the joint, I will pull every string in the book to see that you serve every single day of your five-year term without parole. Do you understand what I'm telling you?"

"I've made a promise and I intend to keep it," Falcone said.

"I want to know the location of the plant . . . the place where you and Masters printed up the last batch before you got caught."

Falcone frowned. "You mean you're not even going to give me a day with my wife and kids before we start?"

"You can see them just as soon as you take me to the press."

Falcone shrugged. "We did the printing in a space I rented at an industrial park. Rick always has me rent the place we use for the plant. He never uses his name for anything."

"Where is the industrial park?"

"I can't remember the address, but it's on that big street that runs past Disneyland. When we were running off the job, we rented rooms at the Disneyland Hotel to catch some sleep."

Holding back a desire to jump and shout, Hart started the engine. He steered out of the prison parking lot and headed toward the freeway. "How often did you move the printing location?" he said.

"Only when we thought things were getting hot. Hell, we printed in a spot in Santa Barbara for almost two years. It was right down the street from the police station. We'd rented a little shop.''

''Why did you move?''

''One of the neighbors complained about the noise the press was making. A cop stopped by and knocked on the door right when we were running off a load of twenties. I looked out the window, almost dropped dead of a heart attack. But Rick was cool as hell. He just opened the door and acted like he was leaving for the day. He stood there talking with the cop for what must have been a half hour. They got along great. The cop finally left and we beat feet out of town. A week later I hired a moving van and moved the equipment to the place near Disneyland.''

Hart turned right at the end of Ferry Street and swung onto a road that ran alongside the harbor.

For the rest of the trip Falcone talked freely about Masters's printing method. It was pretty much the way Hart figured: lithographic plates, a Multilith 1250 press, a numbering machine for the serial numbers.

''Rick likes to do the whole printing all at once. He'll start in the morning by burning the images on the aluminum plates. When he finishes the plates, he puts the plate on the press and starts running off the fronts of the bills. Then he starts right off on the backs. If he begins in the morning, he's usually making the serial number run by that night. When the three runs are completed, I start cutting the bills from the sheets.''

''How many images to each sheet?''

''Three bills to each sheet. That's always the way he prints. Three to a sheet.''

''What kind of paper?''

''Cascade bond . . . hundred percent rag content. Twenty-eight-pound weight.''

''Where does he buy the paper?''

''He usually takes care of that himself. He just walks into a supply house and buys what he needs.''

"Who ages the bills?"

"I do."

"What do you use?"

"Creme de Menthe and India ink."

Hart gave Falcone a puzzled look.

"I buy me a plastic trash barrel and fill it with water. I pour in a bottle of Creme de Menthe and about one bottle of black india ink. I soak the bills in the shit and then dry 'em with an electric fan. They come out perfect. The soaking and drying makes the bills look dirty, like they've been in circulation for a while; takes away that crisp look that's a sure tipoff to the cashiers when you pass 'em."

"How did you ever come up with that mixture?"

"Just tried everything under the sun. I experimented. An old-time counterfeiter named Freddie Roth suggested the Creme de Menthe. I met him in the joint years ago."

The trip to the Disneyland area took another half hour. Falcone continued to answer Hart's questions freely. As Hart steered the G-car off the freeway, he could see Disneyland's Matterhorn mountain looming behind the monorail track that surrounded the amusement park. The peak of the mountain had been painted white to give it a snowcapped effect.

Falcone pointed ahead at a busy thoroughfare lined with garish motel signs. The street paralleled Disneyland's southern boundary. "Straight ahead," he said.

Hart followed Falcone's directions past Disneyland and a convention center. As they entered an industrial area made up of small factories, Falcone instructed Hart to turn left. In front of them at the end of a street lined with small factory buildings was a metal Quonset hut behind a chain-link fence. Hart pulled up in front of the place.

"This is it," Falcone said.

Hart turned off the engine. The men climbed out of the car and walked over to a gate on the fence that was chained and locked. Hart motioned to Falcone. The prisoner struggled to climb over the fence; Hart followed. They approached the building and Hart tugged on the heavy padlock hanging on the front door. It was secure.

"There's a window on the side," Falcone offered.

Hart followed him to the side of the building. There was a grimy window covered by a makeshift curtain inside. Hart unsnapped the leather keep on his belt and removed his handcuffs. Holding the cuffs like brass knuckles, he tapped lightly on a corner pane of the window until it broke. After smashing the glass completely out of the pane, he pulled a handkerchief from his pants pocket and brushed away the broken glass. He reached inside, unlocked the window and used the heels of his hands to give the sash bar a couple of solid upward pushes. The window opened. Since the curtain had no opening, he grasped it with both hands and ripped it from the valance. Light streamed in from similar windows at the opposite side and rear of the building so that it was fairly well lit. Hart stuck his head in the window. The cement-floored building was empty.

Hart moved back from the window, nodded to Falcone to take a look.

Falcone leaned forward to the broken pane. "He must have moved everything after I got arrested," he said, his voice reverberating inside the tinny structure. He stepped back and looked at Hart sheepishly. "What can I say?"

"How does he move the equipment from place to place?"

"Like I told you. I was the one who handled all that."

"How do you think Masters handled moving the printing equipment after you were out of the picture?"

"He'd never trust anyone else to do it for him if that's what you mean. I know him. He'd rather buy all new equipment than let anyone else in on his operation. That you can bank on."

"Would he rent a truck with a lift gate and try to move it all himself?"

"Either that or hire a moving company. He'd use a phony

name. He's got plenty of phony I.D., business cards, the whole bit. But he would never let anyone else in on his operation. Hell, he and I go back fifteen years and he never let me in on anything that I didn't need to know. Half the time when I'd deliver a package of counterfeit money somewhere, I'd never know who was getting it. He'd tell me to put it in an airport locker and tape the key under a phone in a certain phone booth. Shit like that.''

Hart wiped his hands off with the handkerchief, then shoved it back in his pocket.

''Sorry there was nothing here,'' Falcone said, ''but at least you can see that I'm being straight with you, right?''

Hart nodded; they headed back to the fence.

''Where are we going now?'' Falcone said as they got back into the G-car.

''To my office.''

''What are we gonna do there?''

''I ask questions about Masters and you answer them. A stenographer takes notes. We'll be there for the rest of the day and probably most of tomorrow . . . and I have some photos of passers I want you to look at.''

Falcone reached into his brown paper sack. He removed a bottle of Pepto-Bismol, took a long drink and wiped his mouth. ''Can I ask a favor?'' he said.

''Go ahead.''

''My daughter is in the hospital and she's pretty sick. Could we stop by Good Samaritan Hospital? It's on the way to the Federal Building.''

''What's your daughter's name?''

''Rosanna Brown. My first wife remarried.''

Hart lifted the car radio microphone from its dashboard hook and pressed the transmit key. ''Lincoln fourteen three one to Los Angeles Base.''

''Go ahead three one,'' said the female radio operator.

''Request you phone Good Samaritan and find out if they have a patient named Rosanna Brown.''

Hart returned the microphone to its place.

Carmine Falcone rubbed his stomach. "You still don't trust me, do you?"

"Nothing personal," Hart said with a smile. Falcone shook his head.

A few minutes later the radio operator came back on the air. She confirmed that Rosanna Brown was a patient at the hospital.

"I don't blame you cops for not trusting people," Falcone said.

The hospital, a modern multistoried building, was located in downtown Los Angeles across the street from the Greyhound Bus Depot. In contrast to the other buildings situated near L.A.'s grimy and crumbling center, the hospital had a porticoed entrance which was decorated with leafy plants. In front of the bank of glass doors at the entrance was a well-manicured flower garden.

Hart pulled into a parking space marked "Police Vehicles Only" at the side of the building. The men entered the hospital and stopped at an information desk. Hart gave the name to a young freckle-faced guard with thick glasses. After checking a patient list he told them Rosanna Brown was in a room on the eighth floor. They walked across the lobby to the elevators.

"Do you have to come up to the room with me?" Falcone asked.

Hart smiled. "I thought you said you didn't blame me for not trusting people?"

Falcone shrugged resignedly.

An elevator door opened, and the two men stepped aside for a tall woman in a nurse's uniform who backed out of the elevator pulling a wheeled cart. She was followed by four or five other nurses who were chatting amiably. Falcone and Hart stepped onto the empty elevator, Hart pressed the button for the eighth floor. As the elevator ascended, he watched a row of numbers above the door blink on and off in succession. The doors opened and the two men stepped out.

Suddenly Falcone turned and crouched. He used all his strength to punch Hart in the stomach, then the jaw. Hart felt a wave of nausea and pain. He saw stars, then blackness. As his eyes came back into focus he was on one knee and an elderly nurse with gray hair was helping him to his feet.

"Where did he go?" Hart said as he tried to catch his breath.

The nurse pointed to a fire exit sign. "Down the stairwell," she said.

He was still lightheaded as he ran to an open elevator.

In the lobby, he trotted over to the guard at the information desk. "Did you see the man I just came in with?"

"He just went out the front door," the guard said.

Hart ran full speed out of the building; Falcone was nowhere in sight. He ran through the parking lot and across the street into the bus station. The enormous waiting room was filled with tired-looking travelers milling about and lounging in wooden benches. For the next half hour or so he hurried through the crowd in the dingy station, jumped on and off buses, and checked restrooms for Falcone. Finally, exhausted and sweaty, he sat down on a hard bench, rubbed his temples. "Damn," he said out loud. The remark caused a bearded vagrant who was reclining on the next bench to wake up. The man had a scab which covered the greater portion of his nose. "Hey, buddy. Ya gotta cigarette?" he said.

Hart abruptly stood up, straightened his necktie and walked out of the bus station. Back at the hospital he determined that Rosanna Brown was an eighteen-year-old black woman who was recuperating from a fall . . . and that her husband was serving time in Terminal Island Federal Prison.

Hart left the hospital. On his way back to the field office, all he could think of was what Judge Malcolm had told him. By the time he arrived there, he'd decided he would keep Falcone's escape a secret for as long as possible.

CHAPTER SIXTEEN

On Saturday morning Vukovich drove the fifty or so freeway miles to his Uncle Branko's Fontana winery to attend the christening of cousin George's first son. It was impossible to forget the occasion; his mother had phoned twice during the week to remind him. During the trip, his mind meandered to memories of his childhood: long, sweltering days of chasing about the fields with his cousins, swimming in the vineyard reservoir, the sight of the picnic tables burdened with sinful amounts of lamb and pork, stuffed cabbage, roast potatoes, garlicky string beans, goat's cheese, black olives . . . hell, it made him hungry just thinking about it.

When he arrived, he found his mother huddled in the kitchen with the other women in the family. She was a strongshouldered woman who wore her gray hair in a bun as did many of the first-generation women, and insisted on kissing him forcefully on both cheeks. He wandered out to a large pergola near an irrigation reservoir and joined the card-playing men who were clustered around a long picnic table littered with beer cans and wine glasses. He was greeted with rough handshakes and slaps on the shoulder. The older men, including Uncle Branko, a stocky, broad-shouldered man with tanned, ruddy features, a bushy mustache and a full head of hair that was combed straight back with some kind of grease, bussed Vukovich on both cheeks. He took a seat and played gin for a while. As the hands were dealt, there was the usual half-English/half-Serbo-Croatian banter. If Vukovich were to have made notes on the conversation, they might have read as follows:

1. The governor of California advocated gun control and thus was probably a card-carrying communist.

2. The public school system was no longer worth shit.

3. Money-hungry realtors had caused an artificial rise in the price of property and had thus ruined the whole country for people who had to work for a living.

4. The only honest politician in California was the honorable Congressman Milo Dimkich of Fontana, who once worked for Uncle Branko at the winery.

After an hour or so Uncle Branko stood up and motioned for him to follow. Vukovich got up and walked with Branko through the warm and sandy soil of the vineyard.

"What's bothering you today, Johnny? You seem quiet."

"Some things on my mind, I guess."

"Maybe Patti will come back and everything be okay again."

"It's not just that. I've had a few problems at work."

"What kind of problems?"

"I might have to take a transfer."

Branko stopped, stroked his mustache. "Have you told your mother?"

Vukovich shook his head.

"It hasn't been very long since your dad passed away. Maybe you tell your boss at work and he can delay this transfer."

Vukovich ran his fingers through his hair.

"Is everything okay otherwise?" Branko asked.

"You know how police work is . . . always lotsa problems."

"Police work is what killed your father. It's what gave him a bad heart. Years ago I begged him to quit and come here to work with me. If he'd done it, he'd be with us here today. But he wouldn't listen to me. He wanted to make all those big cases. Sure, his name was in newspaper every week and the other cops looked up to him, but what did it get him? I tell you what it got him . . . heart attack."

"If I take the transfer, I could take mom with me. Maybe she'd enjoy a change of scenery for a couple of years."

"You'd be taking her away from her family. Hell, she's been in the women's club at the same church for thirty years. The doctor told your mother she needs operation. She probably didn't tell you because she doesn't want you to worry. You know how she is."

"What kind of operation?"

Branko swallowed, staring out at the field. "He said it might be cancer. I found out from the wife. Your mother doesn't want anyone else to know."

"Damn," Vukovich said.

They walked for a while in silence until they reached the edge of the vineyard. A four-foot pile of black, silt-like material extended along the length of the property line. About a mile away in the distance was a steel foundry with belching smoke-stacks. Branko threw up his hands with a flourish. "I sold the land to that foundry to pay off a second mortgage and three days later they dumped this here. Truck comes every day to make the pile bigger. By the time they're through my winery will be surrounded by his shit. I'd like to get some dynamite and blow up that foundry and all the big shot sonnabitches that own it." He stabbed at the smoke-stacks with an extended middle finger.

Branko turned, looked at his nephew closely. "You have bags under your eyes," he said. "No color in your skin."

"Lots of night work."

"Forget the night work. Why don't you quit and come to the winery. I make you manager. Forget about having to take goddamn transfer."

Vukovich avoided looking at his uncle since he didn't know what to tell him. They wandered back toward the pergola where the card game had become an arm wrestling contest. The men watching cheered uproariously.

"I know you'll never quit," Branko said. "You're too much like my brother. You like to fight."

Vukovich didn't answer.

The arm wrestling went on for another hour until Father Jovanovich arrived. As the Serbian Orthodox priest, a diminutive, pale man with deep-set eyes and a goatee, stripped off his jacket and joined the men at the table, the raucous activity abated. Later, as everyone gathered at the reservoir, the priest christened Branko's grandson by dipping the squirming child fully into the water as he chanted prayers. The baby cried, women wiped away tears. Afterwards, as the baby wailed, Branko brought out a bottle of Slivovitz from the house and filled shot glasses. Standing in the sun, the men drank toasts of the harsh cognac.

At dusk an enormous meal was served at the table under the pergola and Vukovich, sitting next to his mother, ate heartily. By the end of the evening he was drunk and caught up in the mellowness of being in a place where there were no strangers, no surprises. As he hoisted a jug of Vukovich wine and refilled his glass, he wondered what it would be like to come to work every day at the vineyard; to never have to drive down to the Federal Building again . . . no more door-kicking, no more signing in and signing out, no more tedious reports, no more treachery . . .

In the morning, Vukovich and Chance stopped at the office just long enough for Chance to type in the description of

Reginald Musgrave's Rolls-Royce on the face sheet of a blank search warrant.

"What if he notices that the warrant's not properly issued and stamped?" Vukovich said on their way out of the office.

"He won't know what to look for," Chance said.

Vukovich had butterflies in his stomach as he steered through Westwood toward Musgrave's house. Having climbed the hills of Bel Air, he drove past the residence. Musgrave's Rolls-Royce was parked in the driveway.

"Perfect," Chance said.

Vukovich made a U-turn and parked across the street in front of the actor's house. The partners quickly headed across the street.

"Let me do the talking," Chance said as they reached the door. He used the knocker. There was the sound of footsteps inside the house; the peephole opened.

"Yes?" Musgrave said. At the sound of the voice all Vukovich could picture was Father Donegan standing behind the door of his TV rectory with his blond altar boy sidekick.

Chance held his badge up to the peephole. "Federal officers," he said. "We'd like to speak with you for a moment."

"What's this all about?" Musgrave said.

"Open the door please," Chance said.

"Not until you tell me what this is all about."

"Narcotics investigation," Chance said. "Open the goddamn door. We don't want to embarrass you in front of all your nice rich neighbors."

"Let me see that badge again," Musgrave said. He sounded worried.

Chance held the badge up to the peephole again. The door lock snapped; Musgrave opened the door. He was wearing a tattersall shirt, chino pants and loafers. His white hair was perfectly styled and combed. Vukovich wondered if it was a toupee.

"I'm on my way to the studio," Musgrave said. "What seems to be the problem?"

Chance pointed at the Rolls-Royce. "Is that your car?" he said.

"It is," Musgrave said in a condescending manner.

Chance pulled the phony search warrant from an inside pocket. He unfolded it so that the title block was showing. "We have a search warrant for it."

"A search warrant?"

"That's right," Chance said, "do you have the keys to the car?"

Musgrave nodded. "What's this all about?"

"I'd like you to step over to the car with us," Chance said.

With a look of bewilderment Musgrave followed them to the car. "I think I should call my attorney," he said.

"You'll have plenty of time for that after we conduct our search," Chance said as they reached the car. He opened the driver's door and climbed in. He feigned searching under the front seat, then opened the glove compartment, fished around inside. "What have we here?" he said, holding up a small clear plastic bag filled with white powder. He climbed back out of the car.

Musgrave stared at the fist-sized bag, then glanced back and forth at the two agents. "I've never seen that before," he said. "This is some kind of a set-up."

"We don't want to embarrass you by using handcuffs," Chance said. "So why don't you just quietly follow us across the street to our car and we'll go for a little ride."

"Am I under arrest?" Musgrave said, his index finger pointing at his chest. His face was ashen.

Chance took Musgrave by the arm and led him across the street to the G-car. Vukovich followed. Chance opened the right rear passenger door. The two men got in; Vukovich climbed in behind the wheel. Chance snapped handcuffs on Musgrave's wrists.

"I can't believe this is happening to me," the man said.

Vukovich started the engine and drove slowly down the winding road past homes with secluded entrances and high, decorative iron gates.

Chance removed a card from his shirt pocket and read: *"You have the right to remain silent. Anything you say can be used against you in a court or other proceedings. You have the right to talk to a lawyer . . ."*

"I want my lawyer," Musgrave said.

"There's not much a lawyer can do for you at this point," Chance said. He put the card away.

At the bottom of the hill Vukovich came to a traffic light. He turned right and headed west on Sunset Boulevard past more palatial homes.

At the Sunset Boulevard on-ramp, Vukovich steered onto the freeway and headed south. As luck would have it, the one time he wanted the freeway to be clogged, it was moving freely. To avoid looking like he was intentionally taking his time, he drove in the slow lane. He could see Musgrave in the rearview mirror, squirming and rubbing his nose with his cuffed hands.

"May I have a cigarette?" Musgrave asked.

"Sure," Chance said.

The actor struggled to dig a cigarette out of the pack in his shirt pocket and onto his lip. Chance helped him light it. He grunted thanks.

"May I ask you a question?" Musgrave said.

"Shoot."

"You people use informants. I know that. I'd like to know who told you to look in my car. I'm innocent. I've never seen that package you removed from my car before in my life, but I'd just like to know where your information came from. It obviously came from someone."

Chance smiled. "Obviously."

Musgrave closed his eyes as if he were in pain.

"For us this is just a routine, minor drug bust," Chance said. "Nothing personal, you understand. We received information, we go to a judge and he issues a search warrant, we serve the warrant."

"Do you know who I am?" Musgrave said.

Chance raised his eyebrows.

"I play the lead in 'Father Donegan's Parish' . . . the TV show."

"When I was in grammar school I played the part of an Indian in the Thanksgiving play," Chance said, smirking.

"Very funny."

Vukovich took a transition road which fed onto a freeway heading toward downtown.

"I have the right to speak with an attorney. I insist that you let me contact my attorney."

"No problem," Chance said. "Just as soon as we book you and take your fingerprints."

Vukovich checked the rearview mirror. Musgrave swallowed a few times and licked his lips. There was a mist of perspiration on his forehead. "Where are we going?"

"To the Federal Building," Chance said. "You'll be booked in the federal lock-up and taken before the U.S. magistrate."

Musgrave shook his head. "This is like a bad dream. I haven't done anything . . . may I ask a favor?"

"Sure."

"Is there any way we could keep this incident away from the press? I'm innocent, but if I have to appear in a courtroom my career will be ruined. I'm sure you can appreciate that."

Chance shrugged. "Never really thought much about it."

"All I'm asking is that the matter be handled discreetly.

Perhaps you could arrange to have me arraigned in a private courtroom.''

"No such thing," Chance said. "Courtrooms are public." He reached in his pocket and removed a pack of chewing gum. He tore open the pack, offered it to Musgrave and Vukovich. They both declined. He unwrapped a stick, folded it, and put it in his mouth.

"In other words," Chance said as he stared out the window, "you're interested in avoiding the publicity."

"Precisely. If I have to appear in a courtroom on a criminal charge, my life is ruined. Ruined."

Chance rubbed his jaw for a moment. "There is another way we could handle it. There is a way to avoid the embarrassment."

"I've never been arrested before in my entire life."

Chance opened his mouth, removed the gum and folded it in the paper wrapper. He dropped it in the ashtray. "I hate stale gum," he said.

Vukovich steered through the downtown freeway interchange. As usual, traffic slowed to a crawl.

"All we're interested in is your source," Chance said. ". . . the person who supplies your cocaine. Nothing more and nothing less. The problem is, once we get to the Federal Building and you call your attorney, too many other people become involved. Some twenty-three-year-old U.S. attorney will be assigned to your case. Prosecuting a television star will be the biggest thing he's ever done in his life. He'll write a press release one minute after we stroll you into the lock-up."

"As God is my witness, I've never seen the cocaine you found in my car."

"Unfortunately that doesn't change the situation as it stands right at this very moment," Chance said. "You have been launched down shit creek."

Musgrave put his head down, his eyes closed. Chance thought the man might start crying.

"On the other hand, if you want to tell us who you score from we can stop the boat right now. If you're willing to co-operate, we'll return the search warrant to the judge and say that we found nothing in your car. We'll let you go. We do this all the time to protect people who help us."

Musgrave looked up. "May I consult with my lawyer? I don't feel I should do anything without his advice."

Disgustedly, Chance let out his breath. "Fuck your lawyer," Chance said.

Vukovich, feigning impatience, angrily slammed his foot on the accelerator and took the Broadway exit off the freeway.

"Is that asking too much?" Musgrave said.

"We gave you your chance to cooperate," Chance said. "Now you get booked."

"All I said was that I wished to speak with my lawyer. I want to cooperate, I mean that. It's just that I've never been in a situation like this before in my whole life. I'm confused. Jesus. If the press finds out, my career will never recover."

Nothing was said as Vukovich steered slowly through bustling downtown traffic toward the Federal Building. *What are we going to do if Musgrave won't talk?* he thought to himself. He gradually slowed the car down again, buying time.

Chance opened a fresh pack of cigarettes. He calmly tapped the bottom of the pack and pulled out a smoke, lit it.

"May we stop for a moment?" Musgrave said. "I have something I want to tell you."

Vukovich caught Chance's nod in the rearview mirror. At Alameda, he pulled to the curb.

"I was telling the truth about the cocaine you found in the car," Musgrave said. "So help me God I've never seen it before. The only way I can explain it being there is that I loaned the car to a friend day before yesterday. As God is my witness, that's the truth. But I do know of a person who sells cocaine and I'm willing to tell you about it." As Musgrave rubbed his eyes, his handcuffs clinked together.

"We're waiting," Chance said.

"Do you promise that you will let me go if I tell you?"

"Yes," Chance said.

"With no strings attached?"

"With no strings attached," Chance said.

"Are you familiar with a nightclub called the Glass Crutch in Westwood?"

Chance nodded.

"He's there."

"Who's there?"

"The man I buy the coke from."

"What's his name?" Vukovich said.

"They call him Candy Man," Musgrave said without hesitation. "I'm afraid I don't know his real name."

"What's he look like?"

"He's black, about thirty-five years old . . . muscular. He always wears floppy hats. Everyone there knows him."

"Do you have his telephone number?" Vukovich said.

"He doesn't give out his phone number."

"So you have no way of contacting him, right?" Chance said as he gazed at a busy gas station across the street.

"That's the truth," Musgrave said.

Chance puffed at his cigarette. He nodded at Vukovich. Vukovich checked traffic. He turned right and accelerated toward Temple Street.

"Where are we going?" Musgrave said.

"To jail," Chance said. "We gave you a chance to help yourself, but you lied. Instead of being truthful and telling us that you score from Rick Masters, you gave us a Mister X story. Funny, the Mister Xs that black people describe are always white and vice versa . . . must have something to do with prejudice.''

"I told you the truth," Musgrave said dramatically, his voice rising. He maintained eye contact with Chance.

"Fuck you, Hollywood creep," Chance said. "I hope you enjoy the free publicity."

"If you already know about Masters, then why are you asking me about him?"

"Just wanted to see if you'd tell us the truth," Chance said.

"I can't go to jail. I might as well kill myself. I mean that. I'll take my own life."

At the Federal Building Vukovich turned into the driveway entrance. He swung left and drove down a ramp to an underground entrance of the Federal Detention Center. He stopped at the steel gate and used a card key, then drove into an underground parking area. Opposite the gate was a fluorescent sign which read: *Has your prisoner been thoroughly searched?* He pulled into a parking space.

"It's all over once we walk inside that door," Chance said. "I want you to know that. No more deals. And by the way, that door is the only way in and out. There's no way to avoid the news crew. They usually wait right down here."

Tears welled in Musgrave's eyes. "I don't want to go in there," he said.

"I'm listening," Chance said.

Musgrave stared at the handcuffs for a moment. "Rick Masters is an old friend of mine. He has, on one or two occasions, furnished me with cocaine. But the stuff you found in the car is not mine and . . ."

"How do you pay him for the coke?" Chance interrupted.

"He just tells me the price and I pay him."

"Does he make you pay before he delivers?" Vukovich said. He felt like sighing in relief.

"Always."

"And how is it delivered?" Vukovich said.

A green van bearing lettering which read "U.S. Marshal" was driving down the ramp and parked in a stall near the lockup door. A fortyish, paunchy man dressed in a western-style brown suit jumped out of the driver's door and walked to the rear of the van. He swung the door open. Prisoners wearing denim uniforms and leg irons climbed out of the van and hobbled toward the door.

Musgrave slid down in the seat. "Could we go somewhere else to talk?" he said. "Please."

Vukovich started the engine and drove out of the building. He cruised along North Broadway past L.A.'s gaudy Chinatown. At the L.A. River, he turned onto a dirt road which led down a wide tunnel adjoining the dry, cement-coated bed of the L.A. River. He parked the car and turned off the engine.

Chance removed the prisoner's handcuffs and the three men got out of the car. Chance took one last drag and tossed a cigarette butt. For no apparent reason, they all watched as it rolled down the cement slope of the riverbed.

Musgrave rubbed his wrists. "I'm sorry about not telling the truth about . . ." he said.

"When did you first meet Masters?" Chance interrupted.

"A couple of years ago. He was around the clubs and seemed to be invited to all the parties. Everyone knew he was a counterfeiter . . . a white-collar criminal. That was his attraction I guess. You know how the movie crowd is. They *love* new and interesting people. Come to think of it, that's kind of crazy, isn't it?"

"Did Masters ever talk to you about counterfeit money?" Vukovich said.

"Someone else would have to bring it up first. But he'd always respond. Everything was light. Lots of jokes about having green ink stains on his hands. That kind of thing.

Once in a while he'd tell an exciting story about how he'd eluded the Feds. Always kept it light. Extra light. Everyone loved the stories.''

"When did he start supplying cocaine to you?" Chance said.

"It was a fluke. Once I had a bunch of cast people coming over for a party. I was out of coke and my usual connection was out of town. I phoned Rick and he furnished me a half ounce. That was about it. From then on I used him as a supplier because his stuff was super. It left me with a clean head and there was no big jag . . . no false euphoria. I'm talking about some *really mellow* shit. He would never tell us where it came from.''

As they spoke a lone motorcycle rider, bearded, shirtless, and wearing knee-length black leather boots and pants sped south along the dry riverbed at full speed. The sound of the engine reverberated in the tunnel.

"Who are some of his other customers?" Vukovich said.

"Please don't make me get anyone else involved," Musgrave said.

Vukovich closed his eyes in stifled anger. He loudly let out his breath. "Who are his other customers?" he repeated.

"Mostly people in the entertainment industry. Las Vegas entertainers. Movie people. A news anchorwoman introduced me to him. Please don't make me name names.''

"I take it you know Masters well enough to introduce people to him?" Chance said.

"Of course.''

"Then it should be no problem for you to introduce us to him, is that right?''

Musgrave stared at the men for a moment as if he'd just laid eyes on them. "I imagine so," he said reluctantly.

"That's what you're going to do," Chance said.

"In exchange for what?"

"In exchange for getting a ride back to Bel Air instead of down to the lock-up."

"That's all I have to do?"

"That's right."

"How do I know that you won't file charges on me later?"

"That's the chance you have to take."

Musgrave bit a thumbnail for a moment. "I guess I have no alternative."

Chance reached in the front passenger window of the G-car and pulled out a briefcase. He set it on the hood of the car, opened it and removed a statement form. He spent the next few minutes writing on the form. When he'd finished, it read:

I, Reginald Musgrave, having waived my right to consult with an attorney, wish to make the following statement voluntarily and of my own free will: I have known Rick Masters for approximately two years. During that time, he has, on occasion, furnished me with cocaine which I have both used and distributed to others. The cocaine that agents Chance and Vukovich found in my automobile today was cocaine that was furnished to me by Rick Masters. I realize that possession of cocaine is a felony crime but I wish to confess. No promises or threats of any kind have been made to me. This statement is true and correct to the best of my knowledge and belief.

Chance handed the statement and a pen to Musgrave.

Musgrave's lips moved as he read the paper. He shook his head. "I can't sign this. What guarantee do I have that you people will keep your part of the bargain? Besides, this says that no promises have been made . . ."

"Sign the statement or go to jail."

"May I ask you a question about the wording?"

"Sign the fucking statement or go to jail," Chance said. He yanked handcuffs off the leather keeper on his belt.

Musgrave stared at Chance for a moment, then, perhaps for the sake of drama, turned to the cement river. Finally he set the statement on the hood of the car and signed it. After doing so he stepped away from the car and stood with arms folded, facing the river.

Chance picked up the statement and checked the signature. He flashed a grin at Vukovich as he folded the paper and shoved it into his coat pocket.

"Just exactly what do I have to do?" Musgrave said when they were back on the freeway.

"Set up a meeting with Masters . . . in a restaurant or bar: a place that you and he have been to before," Chance said.

"Then what?"

"Then you introduce two of your old pals to Masters."

"Two of my old pals?"

"My partner and I," Chance said, smiling wryly.

Reginald Musgrave took a deep breath and let it out. He touched the heels of his palms to his forehead, pushed them slowly back to his hairline. "When you arrest him he'll know it was me that set him up."

"Would you prefer to go to jail for him?"

"Please don't threaten me. I'll do what you want."

On the ride back to Musgrave's home in Bel Air, the three men took turns making small talk to relieve the tension. During the trip Vukovich's mind wandered . . . he thought of the hundreds of other people he'd seen become informants in order to help themselves. Funny, he thought, the stronger the evidence against them, the more chance that they would turn on their friends. It had nothing to do with the strength of the friendship, just the evidence.

He pulled up in front of Musgrave's home and for a while they sat in the car and answered Musgrave's questions about what he should say to Masters. Finally, he invited them into the house.

CHAPTER SEVENTEEN

The desk in Reginald Musgrave's huge study was covered with what looked like television scripts (Vukovich noticed one entitled "The Angels of Suburbia"). The room was furnished with floor-to-ceiling bookshelves, an antique cigar store Indian that Vukovich guessed some interior decorator couldn't resist, original oil paintings of prairie scenes which all seemed to have a somewhat yellow tinge, a brown leather couch and recliner chair. The window in the room faced an "M"-shaped swimming pool.

Sitting behind the desk, Musgrave looked perfectly ill-at-ease. As Chance, who sat in a chair facing the desk conversed quietly with Musgrave, Vukovich wandered to the doorway to examine a framed certificate hanging on the wall. It was an award from the National Council of Christians and Jews lauding "Reginald Musgrave for his faithful portrayal of a servant of God; a portrayal which has uplifted the moral climate of national television." He walked back to the pair and sat down next to Chance.

"What do I say to Masters if he asks me how long I've known you two?"

"You tell him five or six years," Chance said.

"Where did we meet?"

"Where do you take vacations?"

"Palm Springs, Hawaii, I take a trip to Nice or Cannes once or twice a year."

"Tell him we met in Palm Springs," Chance said. "At a private party a lot of stockbroker types attended. There was talk at the party that we'd made a lot of money on some kind of scam. You think it had something to do with a mutual fund . . . a bank in the Cayman Islands. Over the years you've seen us here and there on the social circuit. You've heard rumors that we were pulling paper scams. We're always vague about exactly what we do, but we always have lots of money."

Musgrave opened an engraved silver cigarette box on his desk. He took out a cigarette and lit it with a matching lighter. "I quit smoking once," he said, as if to himself. "I was crazy to start again." He exhaled smoke and swiped at it. "What if he asks something *specific* . . . like exactly *who* introduced us?"

"Who do you know that recently died?" Chance said.

Musgrave nodded. "I understand. Someone he can't verify."

"That's right."

"Then what?"

"Then set up a meeting. You introduce us to him."

"What's the purpose of the meeting?"

"We asked you if you knew someone who'd print something for us discreetly. We didn't come right out and say counterfeit money, but you're sure that's what we were hinting at. We were very vague about everything, but you've heard from a friend of yours who knows us that we're pulling off some kind of a confidence game with funny money. We've been traveling to Europe a lot. That's all you know."

"Masters is a very clever man. Extremely clever. What if he doesn't accept you?"

"He will."

"Eventually you arrest him. Then what happens?"

"Then he goes to the penitentiary," Vukovich said.

"What happens to *me*?" Musgrave said. "I'm the one who introduced him to the Feds. I will have vouched for you. He'll kill me. There is no doubt he will kill me if he finds out I set him up."

"You didn't introduce us as your closest relatives," Chance said. "Just as a couple of mopes who you knew from the Palm Springs crowd. What he did with us was his business."

"He'll know. He'll know I set him up. Jesus."

"So maybe he'll figure it out when he's in Terminal Island. So what?"

Musgrave puffed nervously at the cigarette. He pulled an ashtray toward him, smashed the butt. He held out his hand as if he were testing it. "I'm absolutely shaking like a leaf," he said, though Vukovich noticed nothing of the sort.

"Why don't you make yourself a drink?" Vukovich said.

"I'm not drinking. I'm on the Beverly Hills diet." Musgrave wiped his palms on his trousers, looked at them, wiped again.

"Do you have his number?" Chance said.

"Of course I have his number."

"Then call him."

"Right now?"

"No better time than the present."

Reginald Musgrave hesitantly picked up the receiver. He dialed slowly. Vukovich noticed another phone on the coffee table. He moved to the couch and picked it up. The line was ringing; Masters answered.

"Did you get that thing?" Masters said.

"Yes, and many thanks. As always, I am in love with the quality of the merchandise. Truly soft on the schnozz."

"Glad you like it."

"I have somebody I want you to meet."

"Who?"

"Coupla chaps from the desert. They're looking for some technical help . . . they're paper product people."

"How long have you known 'em?"

"Five, six years," Musgrave said. "Good people. I met them at a party years ago. They get around. They definitely get around."

"Where are you right now?"

"At home."

"I'll call you right back," Masters said. The phone clicked.

Vukovich set the extension receiver down.

"I told you he's cagey," Musgrave said. He loosened his collar. "He's checking to see if I'm calling from a police station or something." The phone rang. He and Vukovich picked up receivers simultaneously.

"What was that all about?" Musgrave said.

"Just a precaution."

"If you want to get together with these people they'll be in town tomorrow. If you like I can set something up."

"Tell me more."

"All I know is that they're in the same business you are and they say they're looking for . . . a machinery expert. Apparently they're into something big."

"Where were you when they brought up the topic?"

"There's nothing to worry about," Musgrave said. "I've known them for years and as a matter of fact, I've mentioned nothing about you to them. If you don't want to meet them it's strictly up to you. I'm in kind of a rush right now. If you're interested in getting together, we'll be having dinner at Raphael's tomorrow night."

"We'll see," Masters said. The phone clicked.

Vukovich set the receiver down. "You know him better than we do," he said. "Will he show up?"

"It's hard to say. He's the strangest person I've ever met in my life. He might be there early, and then on the other hand he might not show up at all . . . but overall, I would say if he thinks there's money to be made, he'll show up. But he may be very cold. If he doesn't like you he won't talk business."

The agents nodded.

"How did you people know that the cocaine was in my car?" Musgrave said.

"People who provide us information," Chance said. "That's how we'll know if you try to double-cross us." He stood up to leave. "And if you're thinking about phoning your lawyer for advice after we walk out the door, I'll save you the fee. He'll tell you that because we didn't properly arraign you today you could probably beat the cocaine rap in court due to a technicality. But I want you to know that if you piss back on us a copy of your confession will be in the hands of every reporter in this town five minutes later. We'll be in a little trouble at work, but your life will be ruined. Father Donegan will be a Saturday morning rerun."

"Please don't threaten me anymore," Musgrave said as he followed them to the front door. They left and walked across the wide street to the G-car. Vukovich started the engine. "The dumb son of a bitch fell for it!" Chance said, breaking into laughter. "We're closer to Masters than anyone's gotten in years!" He slugged Vukovich on the shoulder.

Vukovich joined the laughter. He put the car in gear and drove slowly down the hill toward Sunset Boulevard. "What happens if Masters won't meet us?" he said.

"Since when has a crook refused to meet someone he thought he could do some business with?"

"Masters is slick."

"So are we," Chance said, his tone suddenly serious. He stared straight ahead.

* * *

The restaurant was a place to be seen. Guests who were somebody—a svelte blonde, the newly crowned Miss America, sat at a corner table with a pasty-faced bit actor who Vukovich recognized as invariably playing gangster roles—were escorted to their table with panache by none other than Raphael himself, a yellow-complexioned young Italian. He was attired in a perfectly tailored blue sport coat and Europeancut gray slacks of a size which Vukovich figured probably fit him when he was a skinny sixteen-year-old.

The atmosphere was one of friendly chatter, with everyone lingering over courses and squirming in cane-backed chairs to get a look at the latest sit-com stars. On the way in Raphael lisped something to Musgrave about *Olivier himself* having stopped in a few days earlier. The room, including the carpeting, drapes and tablecloths, was art-deco brown with wide black stripes.

There was plenty of room at the table. Reginald Musgrave, after shaking hands with a few Hollywood types on the way in, sat between the two agents. Musgrave had insisted on ordering Kirs, perhaps so he could explain that the concoction of cassis and white wine was named after a French priest.

As Musgrave bantered nervously while they waited for Masters to arrive, Vukovich ruminated over the events of the day. It had been the usual rush of prepping before an undercover meeting: setting up cover phone numbers and addresses (luckily Chance knew a detective at the Palm Springs Police Department), convincing a Mercedes Benz dealer who was a friend of Ruthie the Rat to loan them a new sedan for the evening, and filling the car with Palm Springs matchbooks and other such litter in case they took Masters for a ride. In fact, there had been so much running around that Vukovich was exhausted. He half-listened as Musgrave rambled on.

"He's probably sitting outside watching," he said in a

furtive tone. "He did this once before when I introduced him to someone new. He waited outside until the man arrived to see if he was followed. He told me about it afterwards. Cautious to the point of paranoia. That's what he is. Paranoid."

Musgrave smiled and waved as Masters came in the door. He was dressed in a camel's hair sport coat, white trousers and a red ascot tie. For some reason, Vukovich imagined him standing in a Terminal Island cell wearing the outfit. Masters gustily shook hands with Raphael, then headed for the table. Musgrave pulled back a chair and sat down. He set a leather purse he was carrying on the table and smiled. "So what's the weather like today in Palm Springs, gentlemen?" he said in a smooth chairman of the board style.

"We've been here for a few days," Chance said.

Vukovich nodded. As they had planned, Chance would be the one to answer all surprise questions.

"I have a friend in Palm Springs," Masters said. "Lenny Greene. He's the bartender at the Oasis. You fellas know him?"

"I've got a friend in Hollywood named Donald Duck," Chance said. "Do you know him?"

Though a glint of anger flashed in Masters's eyes, he laughed dryly. "No," he said, "but Reggie probably does. He knows all the characters in star town. Isn't that right, Reggie?"

"These people are my friends," Musgrave said motioning to the agents in a priestly manner. "I've known them for years. Please stop being so paranoid."

Masters fingered his purse, looked at Chance. "Reggie tells me you fellas do some island banking business."

"It's an easy play," Chance said. "A hundred bucks for filing a bank charter and you're the president of your own bank. We've done very well down there over the years."

A young waiter in a tuxedo who looked like he might be wearing a touch of pancake makeup came to the table. Masters ordered champagne. The waiter nodded and slipped away.

"Your friend is so quiet," Masters said. He smiled at Vukovich.

"It's because I have a headache," Vukovich said, sounding slightly annoyed. "I haven't eaten all day. What say we order and then talk business?"

"Of course," Masters said. He snapped his fingers; the waiter returned to the table and took orders.

During the meal Musgrave, taking on the manner of a talkshow guest, recounted semi-humorous experiences about filming a TV movie in Rome: something about a mistake in translation which resulted in a concierge ordering up six taxis when only one was needed. Vukovich joined the others in a round of insincere laughter at the punch line.

As a busboy cleaned off the table, Raphael came to the table. "Mr. Masters, you have a telephone call." He motioned with an upturned palm toward the foyer.

Masters stood up and followed Raphael through the main dining room. In the foyer Raphael punched a lighted button on the phone and handed him the receiver. It was Blanca.

"There's nothing much in it," she said.

"Nothing much?"

"Tennis rackets in the trunk and some men's clothes with Palm Springs men's store labels. There were some book matches in the glove compartment from Palm Springs restaurants . . . and some business letters with return addresses in the Cayman Islands."

"What did the letters say?"

"Something about *please forward the stock we discussed* or *the checks we discussed* or something like that. Do you expect me to remember everything I read?"

"Who were the letters addressed to?" Masters said.

"Suite so-and-so on Palm Canyon Drive in Palm Springs. The name on one was Richard Chester. The other one was to a John somebody. John Victor, I think. The company name was Caribbean Banking Unlimited—Caribbean something or another.''

''Any problems outside?''

''No. The parking guy told me I could *steal* the damn car if I wanted. He's great.''

''Thank you.''

''When are you coming out? I'm getting sick and tired of waiting out here. I'm starving and you're probably sitting in there eating like a king . . .''

Rick Masters set the receiver down and returned to the table. He thought the others looked somewhat ill at ease.

Reggie Musgrave checked his Patek Phillipe. ''I have a date tonight so I'm going to run and let you people talk business. The dinner is on me by the way . . . or I should say the dinner is on the *studio*.'' He stood up and carefully straightened his trousers. He opened and closed his fists. ''Bye everyone,'' he said as he left the table.

Masters refilled champagne glasses.

''So, we're looking for some paper,'' Chance said after Masters finished pouring.

''If you've done some things in the Caymens you probably know Toby King. He's been into that game for years. He and I met years ago. It was right before he did his time in Leavenworth.''

''Yeah, I know him,'' Chance said.

''Oh, really, when did you last see him?''

''At his funeral,'' Chance said. ''He died last summer. Do you know Ralphie Sammartino?''

''Can't say that I do.''

''Neither do I,'' Chance said.

Masters sipped champagne and looked at the men, his expression neutral.

''Why don't we cut the game and get down to business?'' Chance said. ''We're in the middle of a play right now and we need some paper. Our regular paper man is in the hospital right now. Otherwise we wouldn't be meeting a stranger any more than you would. So if you want to talk business, let's talk. If not, the dinner's been nice. We'll find another printer.'' Chance smiled sardonically.

''What kind of paper are we talking about?''

''Hundreds and fifties paper.''

''I hear there's lots of that type of product around.''

''We need consecutive serial numbers,'' Vukovich said, his voice low.

''Consecutive serial numbers?'' Masters said incredulously. ''What you're asking for is a very complicated job. Lots of work.''

''Can it be done?'' Vukovich said.

''It can be done. What kind of an order are we talking about?''

''We need a million in hundreds and fifties.''

Masters nodded. ''How are you going to use it?''

''Why do you ask?'' Chance said.

''I always ask.''

''None of it will be passed around here, if that's what you're worried about. Our play involves an old man who is greedy. He wants to launder some bonds without paying income tax. You can probably figure out the rest. The load will be taken out of state.''

Masters smiled. ''So he ends up holding paper with consecutive serial numbers.''

''You guessed it.''

Masters lifted his glass and took little sips, finishing his champagne. He set the glass down and wiped his mouth on a linen napkin. ''I usually get twenty percent for special orders.''

''Our printer has never charged us more than ten percent,'' Vukovich said.

''Separate serial numbers are a pain in the ass for me. And because your old man will eventually run crying to the Feds with his package of paper, I'd have to wear rubber gloves during the entire job. Have you ever tried to work with rubber gloves? Very uncomfortable. Makes the hands sweat. Hell, why haggle over the price? Let's say eighteen points. A hundred eighty grand for the run. I can have it done for you in a week.''

''Make it thirteen percent and it's a deal,'' Chance said.

''Fifteen. That's my final offer. Otherwise it's not worth it to me.''

Vukovich exchanged glances with Chance. Chance nodded agreement.

''All the bills have to have a Chicago Federal Reserve bank seal,'' Chance said.

''That's no problem.''

The men were silent for a moment. Finally, Chance laid his palms on the table. ''Can we meet here a week from now to do the deal?''

''No problem,'' Masters said. ''I can start work as soon as you get me a down payment. I take thirty thousand up front and the rest on delivery. At this point you owe me thirty thousand.''

Chance swallowed. ''We've never paid front money for anything.''

''It's the only way I do business. If you're for real, you should know that Rick Masters won't touch a job without front money. You should also know that I have never fucked any customer out of his front money. I've been coming to this restaurant three or four times a week for years. I'm a very easy man to find. If you want, I'll be happy to give you my home address. My reputation speaks for itself. The simple fact is that if you can't come up with the front money, you're not for real. It's as simple as that.'' His gaze moved back and forth between the two men.

''That's not the way we do business,'' Chance said firmly.

Rick Masters fished in a shirt pocket and pulled out a business card. There was nothing on it but his first name and a phone number. "Call me if you can put some front money together." He picked up his leather purse and left the table.

CHAPTER EIGHTEEN

The agents waited at the table a few minutes before leaving. Outside, the parking valet hurried to the rear of the lot, climbed in the Mercedes and drove it to the door. The agents got in. Vukovich put the car in gear and drove off. Neither spoke. A few blocks away, when they were sure they weren't being followed, Vukovich pulled to the curb on a residential street. They opened the car doors and searched the car thoroughly.

Vukovich slammed the driver's door shut. "Somebody's been in it," Vukovich said as they stood together on the curb.

"Without a doubt."

"If only Bateman would authorize front money."

"Slim chance. It's hard enough to get him to come across with a hundred bucks to make a small buy," Chance said. "The question is, *how bad do you want Masters*?" He rubbed his chin.

"What are you getting at?"

"Ruthie tells me there's a money man flying into town to buy some stolen diamonds. He's going to be carrying fifty grand in cash.''

"So?"

"So he'll be at the airport carrying a package of money . . .'' Chance said. "No violence, no muss, no fuss. If anything doesn't look easy and smooth, we could just walk away. We'll have lost nothing.''

Vukovich walked to the trunk of the car. He let out his breath, turned and looked down the street to La Cienega Boulevard. The traffic was heavy. "So now you want to commit a robbery,'' he said, shoving his hands in his pockets.

"I'd rather call it a *sting*. A little crook gets ripped off to help a bigger crook get ripped off. Two crooks are the losers.''

"And if the sting goes bad? If everything turns to shit?''

"If it starts to look complicated at any point, we just walk straight out of the airport. We just say fuck it and walk away.''

Vukovich walked back to the driver's side of the Mercedes. He opened the door and got in behind the wheel. Chance got in the passenger side.

"Count me out,'' Vukovich said. He turned the key and started the engine, made a U-turn in the street and returned to La Cienega, then turned south.

"Front money is the only way to get Masters to print. Jesus, we're so close!''

"I'm not going to pull a stick-up. I don't care what the reason is, who the victims are or what's to be gained. It's still a robbery any way you look at it. If you get caught you're a robber and you go to prison for it.''

"The money man is a fence. If he gets ripped off he's got no one to complain to. He can't walk into a police station and report losing fifty grand. He's got more to lose by reporting it than we do by ripping him off.''

"That is if everything goes exactly as planned,'' Vukovich said. He stopped for a traffic light at Wilshire Boule-

vard. In the next lane was a convertible sports car driven by
a pale, skull-faced woman whose closely cropped hair had
been dyed purple.

Nothing was said as Vukovich steered onto the Santa
Monica Freeway and accelerated into the fast lane. As they
entered the downtown area, the traffic slowed to a stop.
Flashing yellow lights appeared ahead of them. Inching forward they passed by a highway patrol car parked behind a
wrecked sedan. A young, dark-haired man who Vukovich
figured had been the driver of the wrecked car sat in the rear
seat of the police car. There was blood on his face and he
seemed to be rubbing his forehead.

"With the two of us it would be a cinch," Chance said.

Vukovich didn't reply. He pulled into the parking lot of
the Federal Building and parked.

Chance walked over to the driver's side as Vukovich got
out.

"If you'll go with me," he said, "just drive the car, I can
do this thing. Will you do that much? Just be the driver? I
need you, partner."

Vukovich looked away for a moment. For some strange
reason the scene of the freeway accident was still on his
mind. "When is this supposed to go down," he found himself saying.

"Tomorrow. It's our only chance to put a case together
on Masters. If we don't do this, he'll have beat us."

Vukovich slammed the car door violently. "I'll go with
you. I'll drive but I'm not pulling a piece on anybody. I'll
tell you that right now."

"Thanks, partner," Chance said somberly. "I really
mean that."

It took Chance half an hour to get to Ruthie's. He found
her sitting at the kitchen table in front of a cutting mirror and
a small glass vial of white powder. "I want to talk to you

before you get high,'' he said as he passed by her on his way to the refrigerator.

She set the gold razor blade she was holding down on the mirror and folded her arms. ''Yes, officer,'' she said in a sarcastic tone.

Chance opened the refrigerator, grabbed a bottle of beer and shut it. ''How sure is this thing tomorrow?''

''What thing?''

''The buyer who's coming to town with the suitcase full of cash.''

''You told me you weren't interested in him because he was a buyer rather than a seller. You said you couldn't make a case . . .''

''Well now I'm telling you that I *am* interested in him,'' he said as he fished for a bottle opener in a drawer overflowing with kitchen utensils.

''It's like I told you, I know the flight he's coming in on and I know that he'll be bringing fifty K with him. The deal is supposed to go right down at the airport. Since when are you interested in diamond deals?''

''Who's the seller?''

''A guy I've known for a long time. He's a burglar. A very sweet person.''

''Why would he tell you about a deal he was involved in?''

''Because we just happened to both be at this nice party and he just started asking me about how deals are done, that sort of thing. We were both high, of course.''

''So exactly what did he say about the diamond deal?''

''What is this, an interrogation?''

''What did he say?''

''He said that he'd heard about this dude from New York who was a fence . . . a Chinaman or a Hawaiian or something like that who flies into town, buys diamonds, or gold or whatever, and then flies out. He likes to do his deals right at the airport. He asked me if I'd ever heard of him.''

"What was his name?"

"Wong or Tong or something like that. I can't remember."

"And?"

"And I told him I'd never heard of the guy. But I guess because we had started talking about it . . . and because we trust each other because of coke deals we've done, he's kept me involved as sort of an advisor. Like everyone, he's worried about getting ripped off. He's just a burglar and needs some advice on how to do a secure deal."

"What's your part of the action?"

"Five points. He promised me five percent of the action for my advice on how he should do the deal safely. I figured what's to lose?"

"He actually told you what *flight* the buyer was coming in on?"

Ruthie shook her head. "Of course not," she said. "I found that out on my own. I called all the airlines until I found his reservation."

"Why did you do that?"

She smiled coyly as she shrugged.

"Because you were thinking of having someone else meet him at the airport and take his money, right?" he said.

She laughed. "I considered it," she admitted. "The Chinaman is obviously an amateur. But I finally said to myself, *fuck it*. Why not just make a few percentage points legitimately." She paused for a moment, watching him. "Why are you suddenly so interested in this guy?"

Chance moved to the window, stared outside. "It fits in with some other things that are happening right at the moment," he said flatly.

"You're going to arrest him?"

"Maybe."

"But how can you do that if he's just carrying genuine cash? If he hasn't broken the law?"

"I really don't feel like answering a lot of dumb questions right now."

"I'm going to lose face if this deal doesn't go through."

"Deals get snagged every day of the week. Don't worry about it."

"Not deals that I help put together," she said. "My deals make money."

"This one will make money too," he said softly. On the street below, a beige Rolls-Royce was stopped at the curb. Its driver, a black man wearing a cape and a wide-brimmed hat, walked toward it from the service station at the corner. He was carrying a gas can, then climbed in the driver's side and drove off. The gas can was still in the street.

Ruthie used a straw to snort a line of cocaine off the mirror. She closed her eyes for a moment. "I hope you won't forget about who came up with the information."

"You'll be taken care of," he said without turning from the window.

He heard her chair move. She stepped behind him and wrapped her arms around his waist. "You haven't done me in for three whole days," she said. Her hands slid down to his crotch. She massaged him and he immediately became erect.

"Get your clothes off, bitch," he whispered as he unzipped his trousers.

They undressed quickly, tossing their clothing aside. She moved to the sofa and lay down on her stomach. "Hard," she said as she arched her buttocks. With an open hand he spanked her until the palm of his right hand was numb. She turned over when he stopped; there were tears in her eyes as she drew him to her. After exceptionally long intercourse, they both came. Perspiring and out of breath, they rested on the sofa.

"How much of it am I going to get?" she said after they'd lain together for a while. She played with the hairs on his chest.

"How much of what?"

"You know what I'm talking about. You might as well tell me because if you do what I think you're going to do I'll know about it. I'll be the first one everyone suspects of having set it up."

"You have nothing to worry about. You couldn't have set it up because you didn't even know which flight he was taking."

"You didn't answer my question," she said.

"I was thinking in the area of about five grand."

"Out of fifty? Why don't you think in the area of about fifteen?"

"How about ten grand and my promise that I will continue to not have you thrown back in the joint?"

"Why do you always have to act that way?"

"Is your ass sore?" Chance asked.

She massaged her buttocks. "I like the feeling. To you that probably sounds weird, but I actually like the feeling."

Chance woke up on the sofa the next morning with the phone ringing. He rubbed his eyes for a moment before he stood up. Finally Ruthie, who was in the bedroom, answered it. Chance stood up and stretched, then wandered into the bedroom. Ruthie was sitting up in bed, holding the receiver to her ear. She silently mouthed the words, "It's him." Chance sat down on the edge of the bed.

"Just don't leave the airport," she said. "God, I wish you wouldn't be so worried about everything. Bye." She set the receiver down carefully. "It's set," she said, her voice slightly melancholy.

"What does he know about you?" he asked.

"Nothing but my first name."

"And your phone number."

She shook her head. "He calls my answering service and they forward the call here."

"Then you have absolutely nothing to worry about."

Vukovich checked his wristwatch. Two minutes before three. He looked up. A large clock on the wall of the United

Airlines arrival area had the same thing. The lounge was crowded with hundreds of people who looked uncomfortable or anxious for one reason or another . . . probably, Vukovich thought, because virtually everyone was burdened with something they didn't need at the moment: heavy coats, suitcases, bored children. As the door of the arrival jetway opened Vukovich moved forward into the crowd that gathered in front of it.

He was one of the first passengers off the plane. He looked cautiously at the crowd of greeters as he stepped into the arrival area. The man fit Ruthie's description perfectly: forty, short, fat, long greasy black hair that curled under at his collar, glasses with pink tinted lenses. He was even wearing a loose-fitting resort style shirt like the kind she said he always wore.

Vukovich turned his head to avoid looking directly at the man. The buyer headed down a few steps to the lower waiting area. He sat down on the first sofa he came to and fumbled with his shoelaces as he looked around carefully. Vukovich walked by him and headed to a long bank of telephones which lined the facing wall. He grabbed a free phone. Keeping his eye on the buyer, he pulled a matchbook cover out of his shirt pocket and dialed the number scribbled on it.

Chance answered on the first ring.

"He's not carrying anything," Vukovich said.

"That's what I figured. He couldn't risk going through airport security with that much money."

"He's antsy as hell. Looks behind him every three seconds."

"Any friends?"

"He's alone."

"That's good."

The man stood up and moved toward the escalator. "Coming your way," Vukovich said. He set the receiver back on the hook.

At the bottom of the escalator Vukovich followed the man

to the right into a well-lit, white-tiled tunnel that extended to the ticket counter area. They reached the end of the tunnel and Vukovich spotted Chance sitting in a phone booth, as they'd arranged. Vukovich watched as the man followed the rest of the crowd down a corridor leading to the baggage area. Chance stepped out of the phone booth. He was wearing jeans and a windbreaker. Vukovich joined him.

"Get the car," Chance said nervously. His eyes stayed on the buyer as he walked into the baggage area.

Vukovich trotted out through the ticketing area onto the sidewalk in front of the terminal building. The access road was congested with the usual airport traffic. The G-car, lacking license plates—he and Chance had removed them on the way to the airport—was parked at the curb. He started the engine and pulled directly in front of the United Airlines baggage terminal. He felt an adrenaline tingle on his lips and the tips of his fingers. What if the car stalled right now? he thought to himself. What if the buyer has a bodyguard somewhere in the crowd? What if an airport cop drives up? Suddenly realizing that he was holding his breath, he rubbed his hands across his face quickly, took a deep breath and sat back in the seat. "Fuck it," he said out loud.

Someone tapped him on the shoulder through the open window. Vukovich almost jumped out of his seat. It was a young sailor with a duffel bag on his shoulder. He had peach fuzz cheeks. "Is this where ya catch the bus to San Diego?" he asked in a Texas drawl.

Vukovich pointed behind him. "That way. The bus stop is that way," Vukovich blurted in a high voice. *Please go away.*

"Thank you kindly," the sailor said. He readjusted his duffel bag and continued on his way. Passengers carrying baggage began to filter out a bank of doors leading from the baggage area to the sidewalk.

It could have been five minutes, though it seemed like an hour later that the buyer stepped out the door carrying an alligator briefcase. Chance was directly behind him. When they were parallel to the G-car Chance reached into the pocket of his windbreaker. He moved next to the man and poked him with his concealed revolver. The man's face turned pale. Chance opened the rear passenger door and shoved the man toward the car into the back seat. Chance climbed in after him with his gun out. "Just relax, motherfucker," he said. "All we want is the money."

"I don't have any money. Please don't shoot me."

Vukovich pulled into traffic. His hands were shaking.

Chance grabbed the briefcase out of the man's hand and tossed it into the front seat.

As he steered across a short freeway overpass leading from the access road to Century Boulevard, Vukovich tried to open the briefcase. "It's locked," he said. In the rearview mirror he saw Chance put the gun to the man's head.

"Where's the key?" he said.

"Shirt pocket," the man answered.

Chance handed the key to Vukovich. He pulled off Century Boulevard into an empty lot next to a large post office mail facility. He frantically unlocked the briefcase. It was full of money . . . twenty dollar bills fastened with rubber bands. "It's here," Vukovich said.

"Get out of the car," Chance commanded as he held his gun to the man's temple. "Get out of the car and run before I blow your brains out."

The man grabbed the door handle and scrambled out. Vukovich threw the car in gear and squealed rubber on the way out of the lot. Gunshots. Glass from the rear window splattered into the car and stung Vukovich on the back of his neck as he swerved onto Century Boulevard and accelerated. More shots. He drove through a red light and swung onto a freeway on-ramp.

"Are you hit?" Chance said as he popped up from the back seat.

"I don't think so," Vukovich said. There was glass scattered over the front seat.

"Get off this freeway before someone sees us with these bullet holes," Chance said.

Vukovich swerved onto the next off-ramp. He pulled off the freeway and into the rear of a coffee shop parking lot that looked like it was closed. After looking around carefully, they climbed out of the car and inspected the damage. Vukovich's heart was pounding. Other than the shattered rear window, there were no other bullet holes. "That son of a bitch knows how to shoot," Chance said.

"How the hell could he have had a gun?" Vukovich said. "Everyone gets searched when they get on an airplane."

"Someone must have slipped it to him in the baggage area."

"Jesus H. Christ," Chance said. "He could have killed us both."

Vukovich stared at the bullet holes in the windshield. "What are we gonna do with this car?" he said.

Chance opened the trunk and grabbed a tire iron. It only took a few minutes to knock out what remained of the rear window. Gingerly, the agents picked up the larger pieces of glass and threw them in a large trash receptacle near the restaurant's back door.

At a pay telephone across the street, Vukovich looked up the address of the nearest auto parts store. They used a few bills from the briefcase to buy a new window, then drove to Vukovich's apartment and spent the rest of the day (at one point Chance left and returned with an auto repair manual) installing the new glass. By five o'clock the job was completed. They vacuumed the car clean and replaced the license plates.

After returning the car to the motor pool, they stopped at the Angel's Flight. As they drank heavily and recounted the events of the day, Vukovich had the feeling that he wanted to be somewhere else; anywhere else. For the first time he actually felt like quitting the job; getting up from the barstool, walking out the door, leaving L.A.

"If that sumbitch would have hit the trunk or the doors of

the G-car,'' Chance said, ''we would have been screwed. There's no way we could have gotten the car repaired and back to the motor pool in one day. We lucked out.''

Though they must have had fifteen drinks each and Vukovich felt his speech begin to slur, he didn't feel the least bit inebriated when they finally left.

''What happened?'' Ruthie said as Chance staggered into her bedroom at 3 A.M. She sat up in bed and turned on the nightstand lamp.

''Clockwork,'' Chance said. ''Everything went like fucking clockwork.'' He tossed the alligator briefcase onto the bed. She hurriedly opened it. It was filled with money. ''Jesus,'' she said.

''What have you heard?'' he said as he tore off his shirt.

''The burglar called. He said the Chinaman never showed up at the airport coffee shop. God, fifty thousand bucks.''

Chance dropped his trousers and fell into bed. He closed his eyes.

''Do you think they'll suspect me of having set them up?''

''How could they suspect you?'' he said to the pillow. ''As far as they know you didn't even know which flight he was taking.''

''These people aren't dumb. They could figure out what I did. *Somebody* had to set him up. They know *somebody* had to set him up for the rip-off.''

''They don't know where you live. Shut up and go to sleep.''

She shoved the briefcase under the bed and switched off the light. ''I'm worried,'' she said a few minutes later.

To Chance, her voice sounded distant . . . like it could have been coming from outside on the street. He immediately fell asleep.

CHAPTER NINETEEN

John Vukovich knocked on the door for the third time. Finally, Patti opened it a few inches, keeping the chain fastened.

"I'm really sorry to wake you up," he said. "I know it's late, but I wanted to talk . . ."

"You're drunk," she interrupted.

"I've had a couple drinks but I'm not drunk," he said. "I want to talk to you about something."

"It's too late to talk."

"I'm thinking about quitting my job."

"I just can't talk right now."

The door chain was between their faces. "Is someone else in there?" he asked.

"No . . ." she said, hesitating. "It's late and you're going to wake up the neighbors. Why don't you stop by at the restaurant tomorrow and we can talk?"

"Who's in there?"

"It's none of your business. You never cared about what I was doing when you were working every night of the week, so why should you care now?" A curly-haired, bare-chested young man who looked like the bartender at the Gay 90s stepped behind her. She pushed him away.

Vukovich stared at her through the crack in the door for a moment. He felt like retching.

"Please don't make a scene," she said. Her voice cracked. "It's over between us but we can still be friends."

"You'd better split, man," the bartender said.

"Come on outside, clown. You dirty motherfucking son of a bitch."

The door slammed shut, the bolt turned. Hallway lights went on. Doors opened and people peeked out into the hallway. Vukovich's mind flashed to the scenes of domestic argument calls he'd handled as a policeman. Suddenly he felt as embarrassed as he'd ever been in his entire life. He turned and walked down the hall past interested neighbors peering out of windows and left the building.

Jim Hart made the short trip from the Field Office to Hollenbeck Park, a trash-littered one-block-square patch of grass situated next to the freeway in East Los Angeles. He cruised the perimeter of the park slowly, looking for Manny Contreras. As he drove by a brick building which he knew was a public restroom, a group of five or six dissipated chicano men shuffling about outside stared at him. Manny Contreras was not among them. He remembered as a young agent wondering why heroin addicts invariably hung around public places where they made themselves easy targets for pinch-hungry narcs. On the other hand, as the old-timer who trained him used to say, it was because they just plain had nowhere else to go. He accepted the explanation both then and now.

He cruised around the park again, then drove two blocks east to a run-down residential section which surrounded the park. At a mom and pop store whose front was spray painted with gang graffiti he turned right onto a dead-end street. He parked the G-car in front of a tiny wood frame house whose exterior was weathered and in need of paint. He got out of the car and followed a cement walkway to the front porch of the house. Hart knocked on the door.

He heard footsteps inside; the peephole opened.

"How did you find out where I live?" Manny Contreras said in a slightly slurred voice.

"Your parole officer told me."

"Check this out, man. My parole officer is an asshole."

"I just want to talk for a minute. Can I come in?"

"You got a search warrant?"

"I didn't come here to bust you . . . I just want to talk. If you don't want me to come in, I'm willing to meet you somewhere else."

"Check this out, man. I just got out of the joint. I don't want to talk to you or any other cop. I just want to be left alone."

"I couldn't care less if you have marks."

"Check this out. I ain't got no fucking marks."

Hart stood on the porch for a few minutes. Inside there was the sound of footsteps moving away from the door. "We're going to have to have a talk," Hart said, raising his voice.

"About what?" Manny Contreras yelled back.

"About Carmine Falcone."

"Check this out, man. I ain't no rat!"

Nothing was said for a while. Hart stood around on the porch for a few more minutes. Finally, he walked back to the car and sat on the front fender.

A half hour or so later Manny Contreras stepped out the front door. He was wearing a sleeveless white T-shirt and khaki trousers that dragged at his heels. He strutted to the car and pointed a finger at Hart. "Check this out, man. I don't like being fucked around. I don't like being *leaned on*. And I ain't afraid of going back to the joint. I been there. Check it out, man."

"I want to know where Falcone is."

"Check this out, man. As far as I know he's still in the joint," Contreras said with slightly too much emphasis.

"If you don't know exactly where he is, I know you know where he *might* be. All I'm asking for is a lead. Give me one and I won't bother you again," Hart said as he noticed a weeping injection mark at the crook of the man's left arm.

Contreras self-consciously folded his arms. "I got nothing else to say, man. You can sit here all day. Check it out." He turned and strutted back toward the house.

Hart felt his breathing increase. He broke into a run, grabbed Contreras around the neck and swung him violently to the ground. He pinned an arm behind Contreras's back and snapped handcuffs on his wrists. Hart yanked him to his feet and dragged him onto the porch and into the house. There was nothing in the tiny room except a card table, a wooden chair and a urine-stained mattress. He pushed the man down on it. From the table Hart gathered up two syringes, a burned spoon and three apparently heroin-filled balloons. He shoved the items in his coat pocket.

Manny Contreras was on his back. "You don't have no search warrant," he said.

Hart pulled the chair next to the mattress and straddled it. "Where is he?" Hart said.

"I heard that he pulled a scam on you and got out of TI, but I don't know where he is. Check it out, man. I don't know where he is."

"Where would you *look* for him?" Hart said.

Contreras stared at the ceiling. "Will you let me go if I tell you?"

"Probably."

Contreras struggled to his knees. "Then how about taking the cuffs off?"

Ignoring the question Hart checked his wristwatch.

"There was a broad he used to shack with. I don't even know her name. She's a waitress."

"Where does she work?"

"Check this out. She used to work at a coffee shop on Sunset Boulevard. The only way I know is that Falcone and me was delivering a load of twenties for Rick once. Falcone stopped at this coffee shop to talk to her."

"Which coffee shop?"

"A coffee shop with a windmill thing on the roof. It's near La Cienega."

"What does she look like?"

"Skinny bitch, about forty years old with blonde kinky hair and freckles. She lookes like she might be part *miate*. But check this out. She won't hand him up. He said once some cops were looking for him. They busted her for harboring a fugitive but she still didn't hand him in. The G-man squeezed her but she rode the case and never said shit."

"How did you know that Falcone was out of jail?"

"Check this out. He phoned me, but he didn't say where he was calling from. I never knew where he lived even when we were muling paper together for Rick. It's the way him and Rick are. Paranoid motherfuckers. Paranoid to the max. Check it out."

"Has Masters been in touch with you since you got out?"

"If he wants me he goes through Carmine. That's always been the way it works."

"Sorry I had to get rough," Hart said.

"Huh?"

"I said I'm sorry," Hart said. "But Falcone double-crossed me after I went to bat for him and got him out of prison. He's put me in a real jam and I guess I just kind of lost my head." Hart took a key out of his pocket. Leaning down, he unlocked the handcuffs and snapped them back on his belt as he helped Contreras to his feet.

"No sweat, man," Contreras said with a look of incredulity. He rubbed his wrists.

"What are you going to do?" Hart said, nodding at the tracks on Contreras's arms.

He shrugged, looked at the floor.

"If there's anything I can do to help, I want you to let me know. I mean that."

Contreras nodded. "He's probably with that waitress," he said softly. "Check it out."

"I'll check it out," Hart said on his way out the door.

As Hart would have guessed, there were four coffee shops on Sunset near where Contreras had described and none of them were decorated with anything remotely resembling a windmill. The first one he visited was a pancake house: a stuffy, wood-paneled place with syrup-sticky tables. He approached the cash register and asked the hostess, a chunky brunette, if the place had ever had a windmill.

"A windmill?" she asked. "I just started working here yesterday."

Hart winked a thanks at the woman and left.

The Windsong was twice the size of the pancake house. Everything in the place except the silverware was plastic. As Hart sat at a table waiting to be served, he imagined the customers eating plastic hamburgers and fries.

A waitress came to the table. She was fiftyish, trim and perhaps because of the utilitarian way she wore her gray hair, she reminded him of his wife.

"What ever happened to the windmill?" Hart said.

She smiled and shook her head. "I guess you haven't been around here for long. A couple of years ago some U.C.L.A. kids tied a rope to it and pulled it off the roof."

"Say, does the blonde lady with the curly hair . . . her name escapes me . . . still work here?"

"Marva works nights . . . always has. She comes in at four."

Hart glanced at the menu. "I'll have a hamburger and french fries," Hart said.

"Marva a friend of yours?"

Hart looked up. "Just someone I remember," he said. "And I'd like a cup of coffee, please."

"You got it," the waitress wrote down the order and moved to the next table.

After finishing his meal Hart checked his wristwatch. It was three o'clock. He paid his bill, left the restaurant and went to his car. He drove out of the restaurant parking lot and positioned the G-car across the street where he could see both the parking lot and the front entrance. For the next hour he watched the usual Hollywood types make their way up and down Sunset: teenage vagrants, young men wearing sport coats and jeans, garishly dressed prostitutes, a man with a Mohawk hairstyle. Jim Hart turned the car radio to an all-news station. An announcer who had trouble pronouncing names read a story about a multiple murder in the suburbs. He flicked the radio off.

At ten minutes to four an older model Chevrolet was driven into the restaurant parking lot by a woman wearing a waitress's uniform. As she climbed out of the car and crouched to lock it Hart could see she matched the description given by Manny Contreras. She went into the restaurant.

Hart walked over to a pay phone at the corner. He got the number of the Windsong Restaurant from the information operator and dialed it. A woman answered. "Is Marva there?" he said.

"She just came in. Hold the line."

Jim Hart hung up the phone. He casually meandered to the crosswalk and strolled across the street. In the Windsong Restaurant parking lot, he used a ball-point pen to note the license number of the Chevy on the palm of his hand. He returned to the car and used the Field Office radio to call in the license. It was registered to Marva Wilson at an apartment house address in Culver City.

On his way there he had to remind himself to slow down more than once.

CHAPTER TWENTY

The apartment house was of the two-level swimming-pool-in-the-middle variety that one could find in almost every neighborhood in L.A. He parked down the street from the building and entered through the front gate. In an alcove leading into the pool area, he checked the names listed on a large joint mailbox built into the wall. Marva Wilson was listed on the box for apartment number eight.

Because he didn't want to chance talking to the apartment manager, he went back to his car and got in behind the wheel. He kept his eye on the place. When it was fully dark he got out of the G-car and headed back to the apartment house. He cautiously walked up a flight of stairs to the second level. Apartment eight was at the top of the stairs; the drapes were pulled and the light was on. Tiptoeing, he crept closer to the door and put his ear to it. Inside a television blared with what sounded like a police drama: sirens and gunfire. He stood there for a long time. Finally he heard footsteps. The sound of the TV channel selector. Hart moved to a screenless window. He peeked through a small break in the curtain. Carmine Falcone stood in front of the television. He wore boxer-style swimming trunks and a T-shirt. Hart moved back to the door. His hand touched the door knob; it was locked. He returned to the window. It was open.

A phone rang inside the apartment.

Falcone moved from the television to a wall phone in the dining area, picked up the receiver and sat at the dining table with his back facing the window. Hart glanced behind him down the hallway. No one had noticed him. Falcone continued to chat.

Holding his breath, Hart stepped over the apron of the window and into the living room. He tiptoed behind Falcone and stopped. The room was filled with the sound of a television car chase. "Catcha later," Falcone said, and reached to the wall hook to hang up the receiver. As he did so, Hart tapped him on the shoulder. Falcone jumped backward as if he'd been hit with an electric prod; he raised his fists. Hart sidestepped and punched Falcone squarely on the jaw, causing his head to snap back and hit the wall. He followed the blow with a body punch and the best uppercut he could muster. Falcone was on his knees. Hart grabbed him by the hair and forced him to the floor. He snapped handcuffs on his wrists, yanked him to his feet and dragged him into the living room. Hart shoved him down onto the sofa.

"I didn't screw you intentionally," Falcone said after he caught his breath. "I just got cold feet."

"I guess we all make mistakes," Hart said. He, too, was out of breath.

"How did you find me?"

"What's the difference?" Hart stepped to the television and turned it off.

Falcone stared at him.

Hart removed a handkerchief from his rear pants pocket and wiped his brow. "You're a very lucky man," he said. "I haven't told anyone that you pulled the disappearing act

on me. The prison doesn't know. The judge doesn't know."
He put the handkerchief away.

"So what does that mean?"

"It means that we can just forget about what happened.
You can still cooperate and help yourself."

"I don't believe you."

"How many times have you been arrested?"

"Too many to remember."

"Has anyone ever come *alone* to arrest you?"

Falcone looked at the open window and the door. He
shook his head.

"I came alone to give you a second chance."

"You want him pretty bad, don't you?"

"I guess you could say that."

"If I do help you make a case on him, what happens then?
Will you still get my sentence reduced?"

"I'll do everything in my power to have your sentence reduced."

"How do I know you're not just saying that?"

"Because I don't lie. You're a crook. All crooks lie. You
lie even when you don't have to lie. On the other hand, I'm a
man of my word. But before you say anything else, I want
you to know that if you double-cross me again, the next time
I catch you all will not be forgiven. If you ruin my last
chance at getting Masters, I'll postpone my retirement until
I find you. And when I do I'll kill you. So help me."

Carmine Falcone swallowed twice. "I can't testify. I'll
never testify."

"You won't have to testify."

Falcone looked at the television as if it were on. "I can
show you where Masters does his printing. The rest is up to
you."

Hart reached down, grabbed Falcone by the upper arm
and pulled him to his feet. "We're going there right now."

Jim Hart followed Falcone's directions as he drove from
the apartment to a commercial area in the upper San

Fernando Valley. The windows in the car were down and the breeze surging in was warm and dry: L.A. hair-dryer air.

"What about that location near Disneyland you took me to?"

"Sorry about that," Falcone said, looking embarrassed. "That was a place I was using just before I got arrested. I tried to run off a batch of twenties by myself and fucked everything up. The bills came out looking like Monopoly money. My ulcer was acting up the whole time I was printing."

"I thought you were an accomplished printer."

"On the big jobs I would help him print," Falcone said, "but usually I was more of a printer's helper than anything else. He handled the hard parts, making the plates, the registration on the press. I just did what he told me. He used to put mattresses against the walls to kill the sound. Even though we were printing at night with no one else around, he'd put the mattresses up. The man is super-careful about his business; super-careful and cautious." He pointed to the right as they passed by some warehouses. A sign at curbside read Industrial/Storage Space for Rent. "This is it," he said.

Hart pulled up to a fence which surrounded three one-story rectangular-shaped cement block structures which were made up of separate cubicles with metal garage-style doors.

Falcone pointed. "Unit number six," he said. "Masters rented it using a driver's license he printed himself. I think the name on it was Abbot."

Hart reached into the glove compartment and grabbed a flashlight. He removed the keys from the ignition and climbed out of the car; Falcone followed. There was a button marked "Manager" on the chain-link gate; Hart pushed it. Moments later, a light came on in the office. The door opened and a gray-haired man wearing carpenter's overalls stepped outside. He lumbered toward them in the darkness, stopped a foot or so behind the fence. The ash on his cigar glimmered as he took a puff. "What's up?" the man said in a gruff manner.

Hart flashed the light on his badge. "U.S. Treasury," he said. "I'd like to know who's renting unit number six."

The man turned and looked at the building as if he'd never seen it before. "It's not rented," he said. "He left there a couple of weeks ago."

"Damn," Hart said under his breath.

"Whatsat?"

"What was his name?" Hart said.

"Lemme see that badge again."

Hart handed it over; the man passed it back after looking at it again.

"His name was Abbott. He'd been in there for about six months. Didn't come around much. I think he had some kind of a printing business. I heard the sound of a press coming from there a few times. He never said much. Hello and goodbye. That was about it." The man dug a key out of his overalls and unlocked the gate. Hart and Falcone stepped in. "Hell, you were here with him a couple of times, weren't you?" the man said as he studied Falcone.

Falcone nodded.

"I'd like to look inside," Hart said.

"Sure thing."

They followed the manager over to the unit. He used a key to unlock a large padlock on the garage door, opened it and turned on a light. There was cement floor and nothing else.

Hart walked around the room for a few minutes. Near the facing wall he found a green-and-black ink stain on the corner.

"This son of a bitch wasn't printing greenbacks, was he?" the manager said.

"Do you remember the exact day he left?"

The manager ran a hand through his hair. "It was the twenty-eighth. I remember because the wife took sick . . ."

"Did you see him move the equipment?" Hart interrupted.

"Sure as hell did. He had a rented truck with a hydraulic lift gate."

"Was anyone else with him?"

"He was alone. I asked him a time or two if he needed any help, but said thanks anyway. I thought he was going to break his balls dragging that heavy stuff out of there."

"What did the truck look like?"

"It was just a rental truck."

"What *color* was the truck?"

The man rubbed his chin. "It was yellow. I think the truck was yellow. It might have even had the name of the rental company on it, but damned if I can remember. People come and go with rental trucks every day around this place."

Hart nodded. "Thanks," he said. "I'm sorry if we woke you up."

"I guess I should have figured he'd move the equipment once I was busted," Falcone said as Hart started the engine.

"When was the last time you saw Masters?" Hart said.

"He came to visit me in the joint a while back. He used the name Truman. That's the way he signed the visitor's log."

"How do you know that?"

"When you have a visitor, the guard calls you to the office and they show you the request-for-visit card. He listed himself as my cousin."

"Was there a first name?" Hart said. He steered down the street and turned right at a signal.

"All I remember is the name Truman."

Hart drove through the commercial area, swung onto a freeway leading south.

"Are you taking me back to Terminal Island?"

Hart nodded. "Sorry."

"Is there anything I could do so that I could stay out?"

"You could testify about Masters before the federal grand jury."

Falcone was quiet for the next few minutes. Traffic became heavier as they passed through the downtown traffic freeway interchange. "Telling you about the print shop is one thing, but actually standing up in court and becoming a snitch in front of the whole world is something I could never do. I'd rather do the rest of my time in protective custody than be a rat and lose my reputation."

"Even though Masters is the one who put the contract on you?"

"If I was him, I'd do the same thing."

Before returning Falcone to the prison that night Hart stopped at Trani's restaurant in San Pedro, a family-owned place he'd frequented over the years. He and Falcone ate enormous platters of spaghetti and finished off two carafes of wine. During the meal they talked casually about the money game; Falcone spoke freely about capers he'd been involved in more than five years earlier . . . the statute of limitations for federal crimes.

That night when he arrived back at his apartment house, Hart noticed a light on in Donna Fields's apartment. He found himself knocking on her door.

She opened it. Hart noticed again that she was an attractive woman, her figure set off by a peasant blouse and shorts. She held a book and glasses in one hand.

"Just wanted to see if you've heard anything from the police about the burglary," he said, though he knew that such crimes were seldom solved in a city as big as L.A.

"No I haven't, but I'm glad you stopped by. I wanted to thank you again. It was very nice of you to help me." Their eyes met briefly and they both shifted stances. "Uh, would you like to come in?"

"Thanks anyway, but I've got to be going." *Why did he say that?*

"I'm cooking meat loaf," she said when he didn't move to leave. "Would you like to join me for dinner?"

"Oh, I couldn't do that . . . ."

"I'd like us to be friends," she said, unafraid to look him in the eye now.

Hart hesitated for a moment. "I haven't had meat loaf in a long time, come to think of it."

As she set a place for him at the table, he browsed through her collection of books, some of which weren't out of cardboard boxes, lots of textbooks titled Demographic something or other or Society this and that and novels of all kinds.

"Do you read much?" she asked as she used a hot pad to lift the meat loaf out of the oven.

"Never had much time for it. The wife was a big reader, though; book a week."

At the table over a leisurely meal he asked her about her work and found out she taught four classes per week, had been married once to an army colonel for a few years, been employed as a social worker and enjoyed camping.

"You were lucky to have had a successful marriage for so many years," she said as they ate chocolate cake for dessert.

Because he didn't know quite how to reply, he just kept on eating.

"The manager of the building told me that you've been a virtual recluse since you moved in."

He set his fork down and sipped coffee. "I guess I haven't been exactly a social butterfly for the last year."

"I didn't mean to get too personal. I really didn't."

"I guess I still haven't gotten over my wife's death."

"You never will if you stay in that apartment for the rest of your life."

Hart nervously glanced at his wristwatch. "It's kinda late. I'd better be going." After she refused to let him help with the dishes, she followed him to the door. When she brushed past him to open it he could smell the light scent of her perfume. He said thanks for the nice meal and stepped into the hallway. "You said you liked camping, but you probably hate fishing," he found himself saying. "I know most women do."

"I'm not most women. I happen to enjoy fishing."

"Do you think you'd like to join me sometime? Uh, fishing, I mean."

"I'd love to. Goodnight, Jim."

"Goodnight, Donna."

She closed the door as he walked along the balcony toward his apartment. He felt like skipping.

CHAPTER TWENTY-ONE

Once inside his apartment Hart spread a map of Los Angeles on the dinette table and, using addresses he took from the yellow pages of a phone book, circled the approximate locations of the truck rental companies nearest Rick Masters's Studio City residence. As he did this he couldn't get his mind off Donna Fields. By 1 A.M. were were lots of circles on the map and he'd completed a list of the rental locations.

By eight o'clock the next morning he was at the first location, a rental yard located on Ventura Boulevard next to a bowling alley. A sign on the door of a small office in the corner of the lot read We're open—Come on in. Jim Hart went on in. A thirtyish, black-bearded man wearing a yellow work shirt with his name over the right shirt pocket sat at a messy desk reading a newspaper. He had puffed biceps.

Hart showed his badge; the man nodded. "Are any of the trucks you rent yellow?"

"They're all yellow."

"I'm looking for a man who rented a truck on the twenty-eighth of last month. He might have used the name Truman."

"Do you know for sure he rented the truck here?"

Hart shook his head.

"I don't have time to look through all the rental forms for that day."

"May I look at them?"

Annoyed, the man stood up and moved to a file cabinet. He opened the cabinet, searched through a stack of manila folders and tossed one of them on the desk. "Help yourself," he said. There was the sound of a car horn. The man glanced out the window. "Customer," he said, opened the door and walked out.

Hart sat down at the desk. He opened the file and spent the next half hour looking through a three-inch stack of pink rental agreement forms for the name Truman, though he knew that Masters could have used any name.

By the end of the day he'd been to all the rental company locations near Masters's house. Back at his apartment that night as he copied the addresses of other rental companies in the suburbs adjoining the North Hollywood area, he stopped for a moment. Hell, he thought to himself, Masters could have rented the damn truck in San Diego, San Francisco . . . God knows where. He tossed his pen down on the table, stood up and stretched. He turned on the television and flopped down on the sofa. After a few minutes he realized he was staring rather than watching the program. He turned it off, went back to the table and finished the list.

The next day was more of the same rental-place-to-rental-place. It seemed like every street in L.A. had a rental yard filled with yellow trucks. In the middle of the afternoon he stopped at a small truck rental yard in East Pasadena near some railroad tracks. There were no trucks in the yard, and for a moment he considered driving off. He parked the G-car near the small office and walked in. An obese and totally bald middle-aged man sat behind a desk piled high with stacks of grayish forms which, oddly, seemed to match his elephantskin complexion. "How can I help you?" the man said without looking up.

Hart showed his tin and explained why he was there. He noticed an American flag on a stand behind the man's desk. In the corner of the room was a bumper sticker which had been plastered to a water dispenser. It read *Register Commies NOT GUNS.*

The man stopped shuffling forms and glared at Hart. "I'm required by law to give most of my profit to the federal government. And now you people are here to check my private business papers. Is that right?"

"A counterfeiter rented a truck and I'm trying to trace it."

"Then why may I ask did you come straight to here? This company has over a hundred locations in Southern California."

"I've been checking lots of rental offices. This has nothing to do with income taxes. Nothing at all."

"Didn't I hear you say that you worked for the U.S. Treasury Department?"

"Yes sir, but I have nothing to do with collecting taxes."

"Isn't it the Treasury Department that collects taxes?"

"The I.R.S. is a division of the Treasury Department, but I'm not with that division. I'm from the division that catches counterfeiters. Honestly."

"But you want to check my records."

"I'm just looking for a name."

The man lifted his hulk from the desk. His arms and torso were enormous. He tucked in his wrinkled white shirt and stepped to the counter, grasped it with both hands. "I know what you people are up to," he said. "I've been audited by the I.R.S. for the past three years in a row and *I know what you people are up to.* I also know my legal rights. I have the legal right to defend this office, *by force if necessary,* from any illegal search, seizure or intrusion."

Hart noticed that the man's lower lip was quivering with emotion, his knuckles were white against the counter.

". . . This is my right under the Constitution. And since this is my property I have the right to ask you to leave here right now." He pointed toward the door. *"Now get out."*

Hart turned slowly and took a few steps to the door. He turned to face the man again. "May I have a drink of water, sir?"

The man continued to glare at him as he pointed to the water dispenser. Cautiously, with his head down, Hart walked over to it. He slipped a paper cup from the dispenser and filled it, drank the water. After crushing the cup and dropping it in a wastebasket he removed a handkerchief from his pocket, wiped his brow.

"I don't blame you for feeling like you do," Hart said. "I hate the I.R.S. as much as you do. In fact, sometimes I have the feeling that the people running the government might be trying to ruin it."

The man didn't avert his steely glare.

Because Hart couldn't think of any other way to stall, he walked to the door. As he opened it he turned one last time. "The man I'm looking for used the name Truman," he said.

They stared at one another for what seemed to Hart like a long time.

The man returned to his desk and sat down. "A man by that name rented a truck last week. Is that what you wanted to know?"

Hart felt his blood quicken. "I need to know where the truck was returned."

The man stared at Hart again as if he expected him to throw a bomb or pull a gun. He angrily yanked open a desk drawer and pulled out a manila file. He leafed through a stack of papers, picked out a typing-size sheet of paper and held it out. Cautiously, Hart moved to the desk and reached for it. "Don't touch it," the man said.

Hart dropped his hands to his sides as he read the rental

agreement. It showed that a truck had been rented by Arthur Truman, 7100 Woodman Avenue, North Hollywood, and that the truck had been returned to a rental yard in Las Vegas the following day. Hart took out a pen and pad. He noted Truman's driver's license number as it was shown on the form.

"Thanks," Hart said and hurried out the door.

At the Department of Motor Vehicles office in downtown Los Angeles, Hart learned that the driver's license number written on the rental application was nonexistent, obviously something Masters had manufactured himself. For a moment he considered phoning the field office, but the thought of having to explain anything to Bateman stopped him. Instead he climbed in his G-car and drove straight to Las Vegas.

During the trip, he kept reminding himself to slow down.

Access to the quiet residential street which the church was on was blocked by a saw-horse and rope barricades and off-duty uniformed L.A. policemen who were working for the studio. Vukovich stood next to Chance outside the barricade. After a short wait, a woman with dark braids who was dressed in skintight black leather pants and a fluorescent green halter top came to the rope line where they were standing. She pulled a saw horse aside for them. "Mr. Musgrave can see you now," she said. The woman led them down the street to an enormous trailer parked at the side of the church. She opened the door for them.

Inside, Musgrave was sitting on one of three stylish sofas, a phone receiver to his ear. At one end of the trailer was a bar. He motioned them to the sofa opposite him; they sat down. Vukovich watched through a large window as three actresses dressed as nuns acted out a scene outside the church. Two of the nuns appeared to be consoling the third.

Musgrave finished his conversation and set the receiver down. "I hope you didn't identify yourselves to anyone," he said as he stood up and locked the door.

"Of course not," Chance said.

Musgrave returned to the sofa. "I'll have to give you this rather quickly. I only have a minute or two before an altar scene."

The agents nodded.

"I received a call from Masters last night. He told me to tell you that he liked you and that the front money he asked for wasn't necessary. He said he was going to go ahead with the project . . . that he'd be ready to do the deal by Sunday or Monday."

Vukovich felt his stomach tighten. "But the front money," he said as he glanced at his partner. Chance was nervously wiping his brow.

"Is there something wrong?"

"But . . . uh . . . he said he wouldn't print without front money," Chance said.

"He told me he gave you that line just to see where you were coming from. He knew only Feds would agree to such a deal. It was just a test. I told you he was clever."

"We tried to call him all day yesterday. There was no answer."

"That's because he's out of town and his girlfriend doesn't answer the phone unless he's there. He's out of town somewhere printing counterfeit money right this very minute. He told me to tell you that. That's what you wanted, isn't it? He'll deliver the counterfeit money to you and you can arrest him for possession."

"Sounds great," Chance said without emphasis.

There was a knock on the trailer door.

"That's all I have for you people. I didn't want to talk over the phone."

They followed Musgrave out the door. He was ushered off by the woman wearing the halter top as the two agents made their way across the street and past the barricade.

"We didn't have to do it," Vukovich said as they climbed into the G-car. "Masters was going to print anyway."

"So some hood lost some dirty money. No one's hurt. I say it's no big thing. Fuck it."

"Where is it?"

"I have it hidden. What's wrong? Don't you trust me with your half?"

"You can have it all as far as I'm concerned," Vukovich said, barely controlling his anger.

"That's not the way it works, partner. It's half yours and half mine. Now and forever."

CHAPTER TWENTY-TWO

It was 10 P.M. Hart had already checked out six industrial rental locations since arriving in Las Vegas.

He knocked on the door of a two-story stucco residence for the third time. A woman wearing a pink housecoat and a mask of cold cream opened the door. Because she had a hand behind her back, he figured she was holding a gun.

"I'm a federal officer," he said. "There's no cause to be alarmed. I'm here about the rentals you own."

"Which ones?"

"The industrial park on Tropicana Boulevard."

"How did you find out where I live?"

"I got your address from the emergency files at the fire department."

"Has there been a fire?"

"No ma'am." He took a mug shot of Masters out of his coat pocket and handed it to the woman. "I'm conducting an investigation and I need to know if you've rented to this man. He may have used the name Truman."

She stared at the photograph and handed it back. "What did he do?"

"He's a counterfeiter."

"Couldn't you have waited until morning?"

"I came all the way from L.A. to find him. I'm sorry about waking you up."

"Are you gonna arrest him?"

"If he's printing counterfeit money."

The woman let her hand fall from behind her back. There was a revolver in her hand. She looked embarrassed for a moment and walked away, then returned without her gun.

"I've had nothing but troubles with my rentals. People move in and don't pay their rent. Everybody in this town is a degenerate gambler. That includes the people who work in the casinos. My ex-husband was a pit boss and couldn't stay away from the tables even on his days off. It's a sickness like cancer."

"Do you recall having seen this man?"

"He came in on the twenty-eighth with a lot of printing equipment. I asked him if he was a printer and he told me he was just storing the stuff."

"Which unit is he in?"

"Number three."

Hart said thanks and headed for the G-car. He sped to the location. It looked like the other places he'd seen earlier in the evening: drab, cement-block buildings with garage-style doors. As usual, a chain-link fence extended around the structure.

The gate was locked and there were no lights on in any of the units. He grabbed a flashlight from the glove compartment, got out and climbed over the fence. He tested the padlock on unit number three and aimed the light on the edges of the garage door; both were secure. He checked the opposite side of the building. The structure had no windows. Located at the rear of the building was a large, rectangular-shaped commercial trash bin. He lifted its heavy metal lid and used the flashlight. The receptacle was filled.

After removing his suit coat and hanging it on the fence,

Hart climbed into the trash bin. Using the flashlight, he began sorting through everything in it.

By the time the sun came up he had examined most of the trash in the receptacle and tossed it onto the pavement. His back was stiff from bending and lifting. He reached into the corner of the bin, picked up a large sealed plastic bag and heaved it out. He climbed out, tore it open and poured out the contents. It was paper cuttings. He dropped to his knees and grabbed handfuls of the dollar size strips of white paper. One of the strips bore a thin strip of green along the edge. He held it up to the light. Scrollwork. It was currency scrollwork. "Got it!" he said as if someone could hear him. He quickly segregated the contents of the pastic bag from the rest of the trash. After a cursory search of what was left in the bin, he gathered up the evidence and hurried to the sedan.

Hart phoned the Las Vegas Treasury Field Office and requested agents to stake out the location, then raced to the Federal Building to get a search warrant.

The Field Office conference room, a cubicle which had recently been redecorated with new carpet and wood paneling because Bateman had some extra budget money to squander before the end of the fiscal year, was crowded. Special agents sitting in even rows of leather upholstered chairs waited for Bateman to finish calling the roll. As usual, Vukovich's name was last. "Here," he said. Chance sat next to him.

Vukovich daydreamed as Bateman gave a briefing on some new travel regulations which had been promulgated at a recent Treasury seminar held for the purpose of studying how to cut down on travel expenses. As he spoke, Vukovich doodled some figures on a note pad to figure how much it had cost in air fare to fly sixty agents-in-charge to Washington, D.C. for the one day seminar and return them to their posts.

After finishing with this topic Bateman continued on with the issues he brought up at every office meeting, the reminder about maintenance of government cars, the warning about the letter of reprimand he would write if one failed to qualify at the pistol range at least once a month, the cajoling to increase the amount taken out of one's paycheck for the U.S. Savings Bond program, and the reading of the arrest statistics for the week. "We're ahead of New York for the quarter in counterfeiting arrests and I'd like to keep it that way," he said with the same amount of false enthusiasm he'd expended on the other topics.

As usual, there was a lot of fidgeting in the room.

Finally, Bateman glanced behind him at the clock on the wall; the usual sign that he was preparing to close.

"The last item on the agenda is a bulletin from the FBI," he said. A comedian sitting in the back of the room hissed loudly. There was some laughter; Bateman glared and the room was silent again. He read from what looked like a teletype. "On February twenty-sixth, FBI Special Agent Robert Fong who is assigned to the Bureau New York Field Office was robbed of fifty thousand dollars in government funds at the Los Angeles International Airport. Fong, who was acting in an undercover capacity as part of a sting operation, was kidnapped by two white males after arriving on a flight from New York. He was driven to a location approximately one mile from the airport, where he was released. At this time Fong fired six rounds from his service revolver as the suspects' car proceeded east on Century Boulevard. It is unknown whether the suspects were wounded. The two suspects are described as thirty to thirty-five-year-old white males, both approximately six feet tall and of medium build, one with black and the other with brown hair. Both suspects were clean cut. The vehicle used was a beige late model Chevrolet without plates. Anyone having information on suspects using this MO please contact the special agent-in-charge, FBI."

Vukovich's hands and face felt alternately hot and cold. His stomach churned as he avoided so much as turning his head to check Chance's reaction.

"This is what happens when proper covering procedures aren't followed," Bateman said in his best officious manner. He gathered up his papers from the lectern. "I guess that's about it."

The agents began filing out of the room. Vukovich stood up and mingled into the crowd. Back in the bullpen, neither he nor Chance spoke. After fiddling at their desks for a few minutes, Chance nodded. They headed out a door which led to the hallway. Chance opened a fire exit door on the facing wall and they stepped into the stairwell. He closed the door behind him.

"It's just a matter of time," Vukovich said as his hands massaged his temples. "He got a good look at us. And the car. It's just a matter of time before they identify us."

"Not necessarily. Descriptions are all they have to go on; maybe composite drawings. How many composite drawings have you seen that actually *look* like the suspects? And the car is repaired."

"It's just a matter of time. They'll have a hundred agents working on it."

"Let's don't lose our cool. If they had anything to go on they wouldn't have sent out a crime teletype. They're grabbing at straws. I'm telling you they *have nothing*."

"Your precious snitch Ruthie set the whole thing up. I never trusted her. Right from the start I never trusted her."

"What happened just happened," Chance said. "It's nobody's fault."

"What are we gonna do now? I would like you to tell me exactly what the hell we are supposed to do at this point."

"If you'll hang with me, we'll beat this thing."

"What choice do I have?"

"I guess neither of us has any choice. We'll just have to suck the heat. We'll just have to see it through to the end."

"We'll get bagged. I know we're gonna get bagged,"

Vukovich said as he reached to open the stairwell door. After looking both ways he returned to the bullpen. Chance followed a few minutes later.

It was almost noon by the time Hart returned to the industrial park with the search warrant and bolt cutters.

Jim Hart used the bolt cutters to snap the padlock securing the front door of the garage. The room was filled with printing equipment: multilith press, platemaker machine, enlarging cameras. In the corner of the room was a jerry-built darkroom which he guessed was used to make lithographic negatives. He flicked on a light and moved to the press; there was green ink on it. He leaned down and used his fingertips to move the cylindrical blanket roller one full turn. There, on the rubber blanket roller cover, was an image of a fifty dollar bill. He dug a penknife out of his pocket, then used it to pry the blanket roller off the machine. "I've got you now, you son of a bitch," he said. *"I've got you now."*

He spent the rest of the day supervising Las Vegas police fingerprint and crime photo teams at the location. Three of Masters's fingerprints were found on the press, cinching the evidence. At about 5 P.M. he secured the location. Exhausted, he rented a room at the first motel he came to on the strip. From the room he phoned Bateman and briefed him on the case. Bateman asked him why he couldn't drive back to L.A. without staying overnight. "I thought you'd say something like that," Hart said.

"It's my responsibility to keep travel costs to a minimum," Bateman said.

Hart hung up the phone and slept soundly for six hours. When he awoke, he showered, dressed and treated himself to a steak dinner in a casino restaurant. Before returning to Los Angeles, he stopped by the Las Vegas Federal Courthouse and swore out an arrest warrant for Rick Masters.

CHAPTER TWENTY-THREE

Ruthie the Rat sat at the kitchen table in front of a cutting mirror as Chance came in the door. She wore a knit bikini. "We need to talk," she said.

He stepped to the sink and picked up a water glass, filled it and drank. "About what?" he said as he shoved the glass into the dishwasher.

"About everything turning to shit." He could tell by the sound of her voice she'd been using cocaine.

"What do you mean by that?"

"I mean I got a lot of phone calls today. Everyone knows about the rip-off. People are pointing fingers. I'm worried."

"So let 'em be worried," he said. "There's no way they'll ever know for sure." He moved to the sofa, kicked off his loafers and sat down, leaning back.

"And there's something else." She leaned close to the mirror and made little fog breaths.

"Whatsat?"

"I think someone is watching me."

Chance sat up; his muscles tensed. "What do you mean by that?"

"I went to the drugstore to get some things and I think someone was following me."

"What did he look like?"

"He was driving a tan Buick."

"I said what does he *look* like?"

"He's wearing a suit. He looks like a cop. And I think he's parked down the street right now. Look down by the gas station."

Chance hurried to the window. There was a tan Buick parked in the corner of the service station. It was facing the driveway entrance to the apartment house. *"Shit,"* he said.

"Maybe the guy who got ripped off hired a private eye," she said to the mirror. Her voice was slurred because she was high.

Chance stepped away from the window. He nervously put his loafers back on and headed for the door.

"Where are you going?"

"Don't open the door for anyone," he said as he hurried out. Instead of taking the elevator he ran down the stairwell to the ground floor. There, he made his way out a rear service door to the back alley. He trotted down the alley, jumped a fence and crossed through backyards to Sunset Boulevard. At a phone booth, he dialed the information operator and got the number for Robert Grimes, the lawyer. He dialed the number and reached an answering service. At his insistence, the operator put him through to Grimes's home.

"Is this the Grimes that was once a Treasury agent?"

"Yes, it is."

"This is Dick Chance. We haven't met. I'm an agent assigned to the L.A. Field Force. I have a legal problem that I need to discuss with you tonight."

"Will it hold until tomorrow? I have dinner guests and . . ."

"It won't hold. I need a lawyer right now."

"Can you give me some kind of an idea what it's about?"

"I'm about to get arrested for something that happened on the job."

"I live at thirty-nine fourteen Waverly Drive in Beverly Hills. Why don't you come over here?"

Chance quickly hung up and ran to the street, hailing a cab.

Grimes's living room reminded Chance of a movie set. The walls of the spacious room were lined with what appeared to be original oil paintings (lots of cityscapes) and there were floor-to-ceiling bookshelves. The furniture, including the sofa he sat on, was sleek and modern in startling colors. The coffee table, an enormous driftwood sculpture with a thick glass top, was littered with the handful of sharpened pencils that Grimes had used while taking notes on a yellow legal pad. He was half reclining in a leather lounge chair.

"So that's about it," Chance said "If they're watching Ruthie, it's just a matter of time until they know about me. They may have already seen me."

Grimes moved forward in the chair. The reclining mechanism moved the hassock down automatically. He tossed the legal pad on the coffee table, stood up and stretched.

"As I see it, the only possible defense is to say that you were working undercover without knowledge of your supervisors. You were trying to catch this dope pusher and things just got out of control and you intended to return the money. The problem with this defense is that you would have to take the witness stand. That would open Pandora's box. The prosecutor could ask you anything he wanted at that point. The jury would convict you. Frankly, I don't think there's any way you can beat the case in court." He stepped to a carved oak cabinet and opened it. "Scotch or bourbon?"

"Scotch is fine," Chance heard himself say.

Grimes took out a bottle and two crystal glasses. He returned to the table with the glasses, handed one to Chance and sat down in the recliner again. Both men drank.

"So what do I do?"

"You can either wait until they arrest you or you can try to beat them to the punch with the U.S. Attorney and make a deal."

"What kind of a deal?"

"There're a number of ways it could be structured. Right offhand, I'd say the best way to go would be to offer to plead guilty and offer to testify against your partner. You have nothing else to offer them except your partner. If you choose this course, this is something that should be done immediately. If they already have you identified, they might not go for the deal. Part of the atmospherics as I see it is that the FBI is not going to want a lot of publicity over the incident. I would suspect they would go along with a guilty plea. The thing you have going for you is that no one was hurt. This is definitely in your favor. No one was blown up."

"What can I expect?" Chance said. He had the vague feeling that he was only eavesdropping on the entire conversation.

"Depends on the judge."

"I know it depends on the judge. I want to know how much time you think I'll have to do."

"If I represent you I could probably get you off with a five-year sentence. You'd never have to do that much time of course. First offense means you'd only have to serve a third of the time. With a few other little tricks I have up my sleeve, you'd probably end up doing less than a year."

"Tricks?"

"I have a psychiatrist that will say the right thing . . . that he's been treating you for stress and alcoholism. This should mean a sentence reduction: treatment in lieu of prison time. And if we're lucky enough to get the case assigned to the right judge, things might really go well. There are three federal judges that I'm quite *close* to, if you know what I mean." He threw back the drink; his lips pulled back from his teeth as it went down.

"I need to think about it."

"What's to think about?"

Chance wiped his palms on his trousers. He sat looking at them for a moment.

"We need to make the move now," Grimes said. "If you get arrested before I can cut a deal, you might as well have some rummy public defender plead you guilty. Save yourself the money."

"And how much *is* your fee?"

"Fifty thousand dollars."

Chance nodded his head for a long time. He stood up and moved to a painting of Paris on the wall, stared at it. "I guess I could have expected that."

"Nobody works for free."

"What if the U.S. Attorney asks me to return the money?"

"You can't because you don't have the money. Your partner kept all of it."

"What if they ask me to take a lie detector test?"

"As your attorney I refuse to let you take it."

Chance turned from the painting, moved to the window and stared out onto the perfectly manicured backyard. The swimming pool and tennis court were both well lit; an inflatable mattress floated in the pool. He imagined lying at the bottom of it looking up.

"I know this is a difficult decision, but it's one that you're going to have to make . . . and make rather quickly."

Chance turned to face the lawyer. "When can we get started?"

"Just as soon as I have the fifty grand."

The arrest had been uneventful.

On the way to the Federal Building, Hart sat in the back

seat with the handcuffed Masters. The counterfeiter was dressed in a pale blue Hawaiian shirt and white trousers. Bateman, who Hart figured had come along on the arrest so he could brag about being on the scene when he called headquarters, drove the G-car.

"You'd better warn the prisoner of his constitutional rights," Bateman said as he drove past Ventura Boulevard heading for the freeway.

Masters turned to Hart. "That's right," he smirked. "You haven't warned me of my rights."

Hart removed a tattered three-by-four card from his suit coat pocket. He read, "Before I ask you any questions you must understand your rights. You have the right to remain silent. You have the right to an attorney. If you decide to answer questions now without an attorney, you can stop the questioning at any time. If you cannot afford an attorney and want one, one will be afforded you at no cost. Do you understand those rights?"

"No."

"Are you willing to waive those rights and answer questions at this time?" Hart said. It was the last sentence on the card.

"No. I want to talk to my attorney."

"We have your press. And the press has your fingerprints. There was an image of a fifty on the blanket roller," Bateman said.

"So why do you want to ask me questions?" Masters said to Hart.

"I don't."

"Then why did you just warn me of my rights?"

"Because he's the agent-in-charge and he told me to."

Masters smiled. "I've beaten you in court three times and I'll beat you again," he said matter-of-factly.

"Juries love fingerprints," Bateman said.

"My fingerprints might be on a thousand presses. That doesn't mean I printed counterfeit money."

"You'll have your day in court, Masters," Bateman said in his best command-presence voice.

Masters leaned forward slightly. "Are you really the agent-in-charge?" he asked meekly.

"That's right, Masters."

"Fuck you, agent-in-charge."

Hart tried not to laugh.

Later in the tiny field office booking room, Masters stood slouched in front of a height chart. Hart pressed the shutter release on the booking camera; the flashbulb blinked light. Hart's name was called over the office intercom. He stepped to a fingerprint counter and picked up a phone.

"Masters's lawyer is in the reception area," Bateman said. "Go speak with him."

After ushering Masters back into the office holding cell, he headed to the reception area. Bob Grimes sat on a sofa. He looked sleepy . . . and perhaps slightly drunk. He straightened up when Hart walked in. "Are you treating my client like the nice man that he is?"

"What can I do for you, Bob?" Hart said impatiently.

"I want you to not oppose releasing my client on his own recognizance tonight so he won't have to post a high bail."

"No way in hell."

"I personally guarantee he'll show up in court."

"Sorry."

"Would you do it if it would help a fellow agent? You'll lose nothing. You know Masters always shows up for trial."

"Probably. What are you getting at?"

Grimes looked around furtively, stood up and spoke quietly in Hart's ear. "Chance and Vukovich ripped off the FBI man. Chance is going to turn Vukovich in to the U.S. attorney for a deal."

Hart felt a tinge of warmth rush to his face. "Who told you that?"

"Chance. He wants me to represent him. I suggest you

tell Vukovich. The race to the witness stand is on. The one who loses will get double the time.''

Hart swallowed. Grimes stepped back. "Pardon me for whispering, but I'm sure the Field Office is never totally free of bugs.''

The men looked at each other for a moment.

Grimes stepped to a phone and dialed. "Hello, your honor. Yes, I have Special Agent Hart with me right now. He has no objection to the own-recognizance release. Certainly.'' He handed the receiver to Hart.

"The defendant has made all his court appearances in three previous trials,'' Hart said softly. "I think he is an excellent risk for an OR.''

"I'll trust your judgment, agent. Release the defendant forthwith. Tell the attorney to appear with him in my court tomorrow afternoon to sign the bail papers.''

Hart set the receiver down, stared at it for a moment. He and Grimes went back to the booking room. Hart unlocked Masters and the two men left the office quickly.

Hart returned to the phone. He picked it up, put it down, then picked it up again. He dialed. Vukovich answered. "Go to a pay phone,'' Hart said.

CHAPTER TWENTY-FOUR

Vukovich listened intently to what Hart had to say. As he spoke, he felt tears come to his eyes. He blinked them back. He suddenly felt weak, paralyzed. "How did you find out?" he said.

"I can't tell you that," Hart said.

"Thanks for letting me know. You're sticking your neck out to call me. I appreciate it."

"Turn yourself in," Hart said. "If you like, I'll go with you. We'll go see the U.S. Attorney himself. There's no other way at this point."

"I can't do that."

"Loyalty is not a question at this point. It's either you or Chance."

"Can't do it."

"Listen to me. All that stand-up guy talk is great around the bullpen, but Chance broke the code. Someone is going to get hurt. This is something that you can survive. Down the road, life will go on. I'm going to come over right now. We're going to the U.S. Attorney."

"We were working undercover. We met Masters and he

promised to print if we came up with front money. That's why we did it."

"You actually *met* with him?"

"He thought we were confidence men from Palm Springs."

Nothing was said for a few seconds. "I just arrested him for printing counterfeit money. I'm afraid that if he finds out he was printing the money for a couple of Treasury agents, he'll claim entrapment. He'll say he wouldn't have printed the money if Uncle Sam hadn't talked him into it."

"I'm sorry," Vukovich said in a barely audible voice. "I'm sorry about everything." He set the receiver down.

Vukovich dressed quickly, strapped on his gun and bullet pouch. He left the apartment and walked to his car. As he climbed in he noticed a sedan parked at the end of the block under a street light. He'd never seen it before. He checked the rearview mirror. There was another government-type sedan parked at the other end of the street. He started the engine and drove slowly. After passing the sedan he checked the rearview mirror again. He noticed heads pop up in the car. The car made a U-turn and followed him. He stepped on the gas and made evasive turns until he was sure he'd lost the tail. Then he headed to Ruthie's.

Because of the surveillance around Ruthie's apartment house, Chance entered the ground floor garage through the darkness of the rear alley. The elevator door opened. Voices. He jumped behind a pillar. An elderly man and woman climbed into a Mercedes Benz. The engine started and the car cruised out the front entrance. He hurried to the elevator and took it to the floor below Ruthie's apartment. He got off and used a stairway to the fire door on her floor, peeked out. When he was sure there was no one in the hall he moved to her door. The sounds of music emanated from inside. He unlocked the door with his key and stepped inside. Ruthie stood facing the window. "Those cops are still down there,'' she said, her voice even more slurred than before he left. Ignoring her, he headed into the bedroom, reached under the bed and pulled out the black briefcase. He unsnapped the locks and opened it; it was empty. He flew into the living room. *"Where is it?"* he said.

Ruthie the Rat lit a cigarette with a small gold lighter. ''Part of that money is mine. I'm the one who set it up.''

He moved across the room to her. ''Where is it?'' he said, trying to hold back his anger.

Without answering she turned to face the window again.

''I need that money. I want it now.'' He knocked the cigarette out of her hand. Hysterically she began to claw at his face, struggling as he grabbed her hair and pulled her to the floor. ''You're high,'' he said. ''Just relax and tell me where you've hidden the money.''

''You need me now, don't you?''

''They're going to arrest me. I need that money. I need it right now. Please don't make me hurt you.''

''I don't want to live anymore anyway. My gig is nature and I want the rain and clouds. I want to wear a raincoat like when I was a kid. I want to slosh around in my little boots on my way home . . .''

He slapped her twice. She laughed. He released his grip and shoved her away, ran back into the bedroom. Frantically, he yanked drawers from a dressing table and poured the contents on the floor. In the closet he flipped shoeboxes over and ripped clothes from hangers. After flipping the mattress off the bed, he turned the night stands over one at a time and searched them thoroughly. The money wasn't in the room. Back into the living room. She was lying on the sofa face down. He grabbed her by the back of the neck and pulled her off the sofa. ''I'm not leaving here without that money,'' he said, tightening his grip.

''Lemme go and I'll get it,'' she mumbled.

He released her. She straightened her blouse, then staggered into the kitchen. He followed. She opened a cupboard and reached in behind a stack of dishes. She whirled around with a gun in her hand. He stopped breathing and stepped back as she pointed it at him. "I'm using the money to turn a coke deal," she said. "Now I want you to get out of here and never come back. I'm tired of being used and I want my own life." Her hand holding the gun trembled.

Chance's arms were in the defensive position, palms open. "I didn't mean to lose my head. I'm sorry," he said. His eyes were on the gun.

"The money was mine because I set up the rip-off. Now get out of my apartment. I don't ever want to see you again." Tears streamed down her cheeks. "Get out. *Get out.*"

He backed toward the door and reached behind him for the door knob. He pulled it open and stepped backwards out the door. Once he'd crossed the threshold she moved to close it. As she did so he made a violent cat's-reach for her gun. There was a loud pop sound as his hand slapped the barrel. He flew backward; the back of his head hit the hallway floor. The door slammed shut. He sat up, out of breath. His hands automatically patted his stomach. There was a hole near the waistline of his shirt and he felt the warmth of blood running between his legs. He struggled to his feet and staggered back to the apartment door, turned the door handle. It was locked. He pulled his gun. With all of his strength he lifted his foot and kicked directly on the door handle. The door jamb cracked. Pop. Pop. Pop. Bullets and splinters flew through the door and into him. He fired back, pulling the trigger even after the gun was emptied. Coughing, he staggered to the elevator, stabbed at the call button. The elevator arrived and he halffell inside. As the elevator descended his knees became weak, wobbly, and he noticed his shirt was soaked with blood. The elevator door opened at the garage level. He stumbled out and made his way through the dark garage to the alley. Suddenly he was blinded by car headlights coming from both sides. Car doors opened; shotguns cranked a metallic warning. "FBI, Chance! Hands up!" a man shouted. As he tried to raise his hands he felt searing pain. He reached for his chest.

The world exploded and he catapulted backwards into blackness.

Several police cars with flashing lights were parked at random in front of Ruthie's apartment house as Vukovich pulled up. Across the street a crowd of people, most of whom were in nightclothes, stood watching. After parking he made his way along a walkway to the rear of the building. A uniformed police officer stood at the entrance to the alley, his arms folded across his chest. "Crime scene," he said, "can't go through this way." The alley was flooded with light from the bright lamps on a police light truck which was parked blocking the alley.

There was a sheet-covered body lying on the ground. He heard footsteps behind him. Something hard poked him in the middle of his back. A gold badge flashed in front of his face. "Vukovich, you're under arrest for robbery of a federal officer. Put your hands up or wear a sheet like your partner." He felt handcuffs being snapped tightly on his wrists.

CHAPTER TWENTY-FIVE

Jim Hart sat in the rear of the crowded courtroom.

"All rise," said the bailiff, a sad-eyed fiftyish man whose polyester suit, like his body, had lost its shape. "This United States Court is again in session. The Honorable Irving P. Malcolm, U.S. District Judge, presiding."

The judge, black robe flowing, swept in through the door to the right of the bench and took his seat. After removing eyeglasses from a case, he put them on without looking up. The judge shuffled through some papers. The bailiff approached the side bar, whispered to the judge and headed back to his desk. Malcolm removed his glasses and surveyed the courtroom. He focused on Hart. "Agent Hart, please approach the side bar," he said.

The judge slid his chair to the side bar as Hart moved down the aisle toward the bench. "I just wanted to say good-bye, your honor," Hart said. "I just handed in my gun and badge. I'm retired."

The judge stuck out his hand; Hart shook it. "I wish you the best of luck in your retirement, Jim."

"Thanks, your honor. I'm headed up north for some trout

fishing. My lady friend is picking me up in just a few minutes.''

"The lady college professor you told me about?"

Hart smiled. "None other."

The judge smiled broadly, leaned closer. "You might like to know that I'm going to take your advice on Vukovich," he said quietly. "After all the publicity dies down I'll give him a split sentence. He'll have to do a little time, but the pre-sentence report says he has employment waiting for him at his uncle's ranch. I'll order some easy time at one of the whitecollar camps and put him on the work release bit."

"Chance dragged him down, judge. He's not a bad kid."

The judge winked good-bye as he slid back to the middle of the bench. Hart hurried down the aisle and into the hallway. He almost bumped into Grimes, who had just come out of the adjoining courtroom. They headed toward the sunlit street entrance at the end of the hall together.

"They'll have to call me back from retirement for Masters's trial," Hart said. "I would have postponed retiring, but I know you. You'll get a year or two worth of postponements to keep Tricky Ricky on the street. It's just that I didn't think I could stand Bateman for another year."

They stopped at the top of the steps outside the building.

"I just pled Masters guilty. The judge gave him ten years and ordered him into custody."

"But what about the entrapment issue? . . . I thought . . ."

"Proving that agents posing as gangsters to entrap poor innocent Masters into printing funny money would have been a great trial defense. I could have made Chance look like the bad guy. Hell, I probably would have won the case."

Hart nodded. "Probably so."

They trudged down a few steps to the sidewalk. Grimes shifted the briefcase he was carrying to his left hand. He smiled as he extended his right. ''Let's just call Masters my retirement present to you,'' Grimes said, shaking Hart's hand.

Grimes walked to a Rolls-Royce which looked like Masters's parked at the curb. The busty, dark-haired woman who'd been at Master's house when Hart had gone there to arrest him climbed out from the driver's side and hurried to Grimes. They embraced and kissed passionately. Grimes opened the passenger door for her and helped her in. After tossing his briefcase in the rear seat, he walked around the car and waved to Hart before he climbed in.

Just as they were driving around the corner, Donna Fields drove up across the street in Hart's station wagon. There were fishing poles sticking out the back window.

He waved with both hands.

CROSSFIRE

*The explosive action/adventure
imprint from Pinnacle Books...
the leader in
espionage and intrigue*

BESTSELLING AUTHORS
FROM PINNACLE BOOKS